A Dash of Romance

Sydney Campbell

A Dash of Romance

ISBN: 978-1-990231-18-6

Cover design by abu-chan
Editing by Megan Records

This is a work of fiction. Unless otherwise indicated,
all the names, characters, businesses, places, events
and incidents in this book are either the product of
the author's imagination or used in a fictitious
manner. Any resemblance to actual persons, living
or dead, or actual events is purely coincidental.

For AM, thanks for the inspiration.

Other books by Sydney Campbell:

Temptation - An Allie Styles Romance (Book 1)
Deception - An Allie Styles Romance (Book 2)
Reckonings - An Allie Styles Romance (Book 3)
Beginnings - An Allie Styles Romance (Book 4)

The Allie Styles Romance Boxed Set

*Reawakening - Courtyard Tales of
Contemporary Romance (Book 1)*
*Redemption - Courtyard Tales of Contemporary
Romance (Book 2)*
*Reckless - Courtyard Tales of Contemporary
Romance (Book 3)*

*Acting out of Love - Mountain Valley Romance
(Book 1)*
*No Reservations Required - Mountain Valley
Romance (Book 2)*
*A Dash of Romance - Mountain Valley
Romance (Book 3)*
*Coming Around Again - Mountain Valley
Romance (Book 4)*
Last Call - Mountain Valley Romance (Book 5)

CHAPTER ONE

Maggie

I was tucking the fitted sheet under the mattress in room 219 when Audra, my supervisor, stuck her head in the door.

"Hey, Mags, you almost done on this floor?" she asked.

"Yeah," I said, straightening up. "I've got two more rooms and I'm done. What's up?"

"Trashed room on three. I was hoping you could get to it before noon?"

I nodded, checking the time on my phone. Satisfied, Audra retreated and left me to my work.

It was early May and I was three weeks into my job on the housekeeping staff at The Elway hotel in Mountain Valley. I'd gotten the job through my brother, Justin, who owned a restaurant a few towns over. I'd called him two months ago, begging him to find me something, anything, that would get me out of the city.

Mountain Valley was small, but friendly and scenic. Everyone seemed to know everybody. It was a quiet little haven for part of the year, but really came alive in the summer and winter months when it was overrun by tourists and cottagers. Over the past year, movie star Mason Scott had started building a production studio in one of the old abandoned warehouses, and that was bringing in a whole different clientele.

Which brought me back to the trashed room on the third floor. I'd been in town less than a month, but already I'd spotted quite a few big stars coming in and out of the hotel. They were the kinds of guests a small town wasn't used to, and everyone was still trying to figure out how to navigate the change. I found it amusing, coming from the city and having a much different perspective on celebrities, but in the end, it meant a busier summer for the hotel and an increased need for staff. So there I was.

The work itself didn't bother me—changing sheets, cleaning bathtubs, scrubbing toilets. It was mindless, and that was exactly what I was looking for, something that would pay the bills but not take up any mental space, leaving me free to write in the evenings. That was all I wanted, to be left alone in peace while I wrote my novel.

I finished dusting, left the room, and was getting ready to tackle the last two when I felt my phone buzz in my pocket. I pulled it out and saw a text message from, of all people, my mother.

Sweetheart. We're coming for a visit. Be there June 2. Can't wait to see you.

CHAPTER TWO

Liam

My alarm was going off much too early. I opened my eyes, letting them adjust to the darkness in the room. Slowly, the forest green walls came into view, along with the framed portraits that hung on my bedroom wall. I turned and saw the vague outline of a body in bed beside me, then turned to find my phone.

It wasn't my alarm. Who the fuck was calling me on a Sunday morning?

"This better be really fucking good," I said.

"Liam? Justin. Was wondering if you could swing by this morning."

I sat up in bed, despite the sounds of protest from Piper, the woman on my right. I put my hand on her hip to soothe her, running it over the curve of her ass. Justin owned one of the hottest restaurants in Rocky Heights, a resort town twenty kilometres down the highway. This past winter, I'd kind of stolen his sous-chef, Toni, to come work at my restaurant, Cagney's, in Mountain Valley. Well, Adam's restaurant, really, but as executive chef, I considered it mine, too.

"Yeah, sure thing. What's up buddy?" I asked.

"We'll talk when you get here. Don't stop for coffee."

Shit. I hung up the phone, then leaned over to kiss Piper's cheek, hoping I wasn't about to piss her off. She rolled over and looked at me.

"Listen, Pipes, I'm really sorry but I've got to run."

I stood up and pulled on a pair of jeans and a T-shirt that smelled okay. Then I ran my hands through my hair before heading to the bathroom to brush my teeth. When I came back, she was still lounging, naked, in my bed. It was very hard to leave.

"You mad?" I asked.

"Not at all," she said. "Just taking a minute to get moving. That a new tattoo?"

"Which one?" I asked.

"Lower bicep," she said.

I flexed my arm to show off the tattoo, eliciting a smile.

"You're welcome to hang here until I get back," I suggested.

She shot me a sympathetic smile.

"Liam. Last night was great and all, but I'm not really one to stick around."

I walked over and slapped her on the ass.

"Just remember to lock up when you leave."

*

Thirty minutes later, I was sitting in Justin's restaurant, nursing a cup of steaming hot coffee.

"So," he said. "How's it working out with Toni?"

"Great, man. I can't thank you enough for letting us steal her away. I don't know how I can ever repay you."

"Funny you should mention that."

A cold chill went down my back.

"Anything, man. Seriously. What is it?"

Justin put down his cup and leaned across the table.

"My sister is working in that little boutique hotel in Mountain Valley, you know the one?"

"The Elway?" I said.

"That's it. Anyway, she's a writer, wanted to get out of the city, and so I found her a job that would support her while she worked on her

9

novel."

"I didn't know you had a sister."

"There's a lot you don't know about me. Now shut up and listen."

I took a sip of coffee.

"My folks are coming for a visit early June. That's three weeks away. They bought an RV and they're touring Canada. They're pissed that Maggie moved out here, and at her age, they think it's time she get serious and settle down. They want her to come home. So they threatened to find her a husband."

I spit out my coffee.

"Excuse me?"

He waved me off.

"It's not as medieval as it sounds. A family friend they want to set her up with. So she panicked and lied, told them she was seeing someone. And now they're coming to check him out."

"Wow. That sucks. What is she going to do?"

Justin stared at me like I was slow, and that's when it sank in.

"Oh. Shit. You want me to play the boyfriend?" I asked.

"I do."

"For how long?"

"One week."

I swallowed and thought about it. Toni was a great fucking sous-chef.

"She doesn't have any friends that can do this?" I asked.

"She's been living here for three weeks. She doesn't have any friends at all. And you're the only one who owes me a favour."

"Huh."

"There's one catch."

I looked up, still trying to figure a way out of this.

"What's that?" I asked.

"You can't touch her. She's my sister."

"Well then why the hell would you ask me? I sleep with everything that moves. Or haven't you heard?"

"I'm asking you because I know you'll do it. And you'll do it because if you don't, I'll offer Toni the executive chef position here."

"Justin—"

"I'm not fucking kidding, Liam. She's my sister, and I'll do anything for her."

"And knowing what a dog I am, you still trust me with her?"

"I do. Knowing what a dog you are, you're the only one I trust not to fall for her."

*

11

Three mornings later, I found myself sitting in a booth at my favourite roadside diner, nursing another cup of coffee and a massive hangover. The night before, it had been our bartender, Bree's, birthday, and we'd stayed late to celebrate. Bree mixed a mean cocktail and before long we were all pretty drunk.

I was contemplating the toast and fried egg on my plate when I a shadow fell across the table. I glanced up and saw a cute redhead, hair tied back, with bright green eyes. Wearing no make-up, she was dressed in jeans, a sweatshirt, and a pair of running shoes.

"Sorry," I mumbled, turning back to my eggs. "I'm actually waiting for someone."

"Liam?" she said.

My head snapped back up and I looked at her again.

"Maggie?" I asked.

She nodded, relieved, and pointed awkwardly to the bench across from me. I sat up straighter and motioned for her to sit down.

"Yes, please, sit. I'm so sorry. I was expecting a female version of your ugly-ass brother. You're actually kind of cute."

She blushed furiously, which oddly charming. Clearing her throat, she reached her hand across the table.

"I really want to thank you for agreeing to

do this," she said.

I took her hand and shook it.

"No problem. Really. I owe your brother big time. Happy to help."

She nodded, then pulled a notebook out of her bag and flipped through the pages.

"So, there are a couple of things," she said, finding her page and running her finger down a list.

"Yes…?"

"Well, you know my parents are coming on June 2, right? That's in about three weeks. I figure maybe we should get together a few times before then, or at least talk on the phone, so we're not so awkward around them?"

Awkward?

"Yeah. Sure. Whatever you want."

"Great. We should really get to know each other. My parents are really good at the third degree."

The waitress came over and Maggie smiled up at her. Without having opened her menu, she recited her order.

"I'll have two eggs, scrambled, well-done, bacon crispy, double the potatoes, whole wheat toast, and I notice you don't have any strawberry jam in the basket. Can you please bring some with the order?"

The waitress wrote everything down,

nodding.

"Oh! And an orange juice instead of coffee, please. Thanks."

I watched her, impressed. As a chef, I had a healthy appreciation for people who liked to eat. She clearly liked to eat. I pushed my plate aside.

"All right, then. What are you doing in Mountain Valley?"

She looked up from her notebook, perhaps confused that I'd gone off-script.

"Excuse me?"

"Well, if we're dating, and I gather pretty seriously, I'd certainly know why you moved out here."

She smiled and relaxed a bit.

"Right. Of course. I'm a writer. I wanted to get away from home, somewhere quiet, and finish my novel. Justin hooked me up with this housekeeping gig, which is great because it pays well, the hours are perfect, and it doesn't sap my mental energy during the day."

I nodded, taking her in. She *was* cute. I hadn't been lying about that. Fresh-faced. Scrubbed. All those "good girl" adjectives.

"What kind of novel are you writing?" I asked before taking a sip of my coffee.

"Romance," she said.

I almost choked. In my mind, romance

writers wore black and showed cleavage. Sitting across from me was the exact opposite of that. She was wholesomeness wrapped up with a bow.

"You write romance novels?" I instantly regretted my incredulous tone.

She set aside her notebook as the waitress returned with her food. After she left, Maggie took her time digging in before responding to my question.

"Well, a novel. And it's not done yet. But yes, I write romance. That amuses you?"

"Damn straight it does."

"Why?"

"Because those things are pure fantasy. The only thing real is what's in front of you in the moment. Attraction, chemistry, sex."

She cleared her throat and shifted on the bench. I was enjoying watching her squirm.

"Maybe we should change the subject," she said. "My brother tells me you're a chef. Where do you work?"

"Cagney's."

"And do you like it?"

"Love it. Nowhere I'd rather be. I think maybe I should read this novel of yours."

Her fork was halfway to her mouth and she blushed again, that deep crimson that tickled me so much earlier. She put her fork back down on her plate and wiped her mouth with her napkin.

"It's not ready."

"I realize that, but if we're so serious, doesn't it make sense I'd have read your book? I mean, I'm sure your folks will ask about it."

"No one has read it."

I rolled my eyes.

"Don't worry. I'm no one. A month from now, I'll be out of your life and you'll never have to see me again. Let me read the damn book."

In truth, she could've just outlined the basic plot and that would have been fine. But I was fucking dying of curiosity to see what kind of romance writing this woman was doing. Justin had warned me not to touch her, but that was the furthest thing from my mind. I felt like if I laid a hand on her I'd be sullying her somehow. She was just that good.

"How old are you?" she asked.

"Thirty-two. You?"

"Twenty-seven."

She looked younger. I was relieved, but I wasn't sure why. Still couldn't figure out why her folks were so concerned. She was still a baby. When Justin had said 'at her age,' I figured she was older than he was, and he was pushing forty.

She polished off her breakfast, placing her cutlery together at four o'clock. Whatever else, she was certainly raised with manners. She glanced over at her notebook, licked her lip nervously, and glanced over at me for a second before averting her eyes.

"There's, uh, one more thing," she said, barely audible.

"Yeah? What's that?"

"Um, I kind of told my parents we were living together."

I raised my eyebrow. This was getting interesting.

"Well, that shouldn't be a problem. You've got a guest room, right? It's only a week."

"I do have a guest room." She paused. "My parents are staying in it."

Ah.

"So, you're telling me I have to sleep in your bedroom for a week?" I asked, amused at how uncomfortable she was.

"Yeah. I'll sleep on the floor, don't worry, it's just—"

"You know what, it's fine."

"Really?"

"Yeah. I have some renovation work that needs to get done at my house. If I'm out for a week, the contractor can get in and have free reign. This works out perfectly."

"Liam, I can't thank you enough. Seriously. I owe you."

"No, actually, you don't. The only reason I'm here is because I owed your brother."

CHAPTER THREE

Maggie

"I realize that," I said. "And I'm really grateful. I guess that's all I'm trying to say."

I reached into my lap and fiddled with my napkin. The man sitting across the table was easily over six feet tall. He was broader than anyone I'd ever seen up close, and he was covered in tattoos—sleeves down both arms. His hair was dark and cropped close, almost like a buzz-cut.

I had been apprehensive about this whole arrangement to begin with, but my worry solidified when I saw Liam. As I sat across from him, eating my breakfast and trying to answer his questions at the same time, I tried to figure out how I could get my parents to believe that I had ended up with him.

I mean, he wasn't bad-looking. In fact, when you got down to it, he was pretty hot. But he was definitely not my type. My type would probably wear a sweater vest. Not that I even knew for sure. I guess that's why I got so defensive when he acted so surprised that I write romance. How many romance writers don't even know who their ideal partner is?

I spent the entire meal in a sweat, trying to figure out how to bring up the whole 'living together' thing. It was a crazy plan, but it was the only way to get my parents off my back. I longed for the days when they were warning me not to spend the night with a guy. The past few years had been all about, 'when are you going to settle down with someone?' Talk about mixed messages.

The relief I felt when he agreed so easily set me at ease. The more I thought about it, the more Liam looked like a great choice after all. He had a solid, respectable career and no divorces. Maybe his appearance would be so off-putting to my parents they'd either flee or be so disappointed in me they gave up altogether.

"Your brother tells me you're working at The Elway," he said, reaching for the bill.

"Yeah. Housekeeping. I can get that. I ate more than you did," I said.

"Nah, don't sweat it." He pulled out his wallet and left a twenty on the table.

"So, when are you, um, free to maybe talk, or meet, you know? So we can, uh, get to know each other?" I asked.

A slow, lazy smile spread across his face. It made me uneasy as he studied me.

"Why don't you send me your book, and when I finish reading, I'll text you and we'll set something up."

I laughed and stood up, grabbing my bag.

"Sure. That sounds great."

He stood and looked me up and down. I was a good six inches shorter than he was, my frame much tinier. We looked ridiculous standing there together, him in black and tattoos, me looking like a college student. I shifted from one foot to another, unsure what to do. I reached out my hand again, awkwardly. He laughed and pulled me in for a hug.

"Better get used to a little PDA," he whispered before slapping me lightly on the back and walking out the front door.

*

A couple of days later, I was getting room 325 ready for check-in when I felt my phone buzz in my pocket. I pulled it out and saw a text message from Tammy at reception.

Your boyfriend's looking for you. I sent him up to the third floor. He's HOT!!!

My boyfriend? I panicked for a moment, checking my reflection in the mirror. I was neat, but I looked like a maid. What the hell was Liam doing here? And why was he calling himself my boyfriend?

I heard him long before I saw him down the hall, calling out my name. I rushed to the door and stuck my head out, putting up my finger in the universal sign for shut the fuck up. He broke into a jog when he saw me, grabbing my elbow and steering me back into the room.

"What are you doing here? And why did you tell Tammy you're my boyfriend?"

"Getting into character. But that's beside the point."

I stared at him.

"What's the point?"

He grabbed me by both shoulders and looked straight into my eyes.

"Where's the sex?"

I just stood there, blinking.

He let go of me and started to pace, throwing his hands up in air every so often as he spoke, emphasizing his frustration.

"I mean, we've got a guy and a girl, they're

clearly hot for each other, and every time something's about to go down, the goddamn door closes. What the fuck is up with that?"

I cleared my throat.

"Well, I write clean romance."

"Who the fuck reads clean romance?" he hissed. "Women read this shit to get off, don't they? It's lady porn."

I bristled at his description and was about to argue with him when I decided there was no point. He obviously wouldn't get it.

"Some people prefer clean romance. Sex isn't for everyone."

"Sex is for everyone," he roared, incredulous.

"It's not for me."

He stopped pacing and his jaw dropped to the floor. Gobsmacked was the only expression that described him at that moment.

"You've never had sex?" he whispered.

"Of course I have!" I replied, indignant. "I just don't particularly enjoy it."

He sat down heavily on the bed. I silently cursed the fact I'd have to redo the bedspread but figured that was small potatoes in the relative scheme of things. He patted the space beside him.

"Sit. I need you to explain this to me."

I walked over to the door and glanced out

the hall, closing the door partway as I walked back to join him on the bed.

"What's there to explain?" I said. "Some people like sex, some people don't. I fall into the latter camp."

He shook his head.

"I don't get it. Are you, like, asexual or something?"

I thought about it.

"No. Sex just doesn't do it for me. In fact, I really don't see what all the fuss is about. I'm pretty convinced that most women lie about their sexual experiences. This is why I write clean romance. I *know* there are women out there who don't enjoy reading about sex because I'm one of them."

Liam looked at me, then looked out across the room, staring at our reflections in the mirror over the dresser.

"So you're telling me I'm about to fake date a woman who hates men."

"I do not hate men."

"I'll have to take your word on that." He paused. "Your parents are going to buy this?"

"I hope so."

He reached out to take my hand and I pulled back, shocked.

"Yeah, I don't think they're going to buy this."

He turned towards me, tucking one long leg up underneath him as he stared into my eyes.

"Here's the thing. I made a vow to your brother not to touch you—"

Mortified, I started to interrupt him, but he put his hand out to stop me.

"I'm telling you this so you know you don't have to worry. I am not going to make a move on you. I promise. Especially after that confession. But I am going to have to do things when your parents are around."

"Like what kind of things?"

He reached out to tuck a stray lock of hair behind my ear. Again, I jumped back.

"Things like that," he said. "I'm going to hold your hand. I'm going to kiss you. You want your parents to believe we're living together? We're going to have to look like we're intimate."

I took a deep breath. This was something I hadn't considered.

"If this is going to work, you're going to have to get comfortable with me. So screw these phone conversations you had in mind. We've got a few weeks? Let's take some walks in public. Go out to eat together. You'll learn I'm not a monster, and when I go to take your hand, you'll let me."

CHAPTER FOUR

Liam

A couple of days later, I stopped by the hotel to pick Maggie up from work. I had a lull in the afternoon and I told Adam I had a few errands to run.

I caught her by the reception desk, and she looked surprised to see me. I doubted my plan, unsure why I was putting any effort into this. All I had to do was show up.

The woman at reception eyed me up and down before smiling. I smiled back, politely, but she definitely wasn't my type. Besides, Maggie.

"Bye, Mags. See you tomorrow," she called as we turned to leave.

I placed my hand on the small of Maggie's back, and while I felt her stiffen, she didn't cringe or shy away. Progress. As we exited onto the sidewalk, I turned to her.

"They call you Mags?" I asked.

"Yeah, it's my nickname. Why?"

I shook my head.

"Doesn't suit you. I'll come up with something better."

She stopped and stared at me.

"It doesn't suit me?"

"Nope. Come, let's go. I don't have much time."

I led her across the street, through the town square, and towards a hiking path that cut a flat trail through the forest, leading to the public beach. She kept up my quick pace, but I slowed as we approached the trailhead.

"Let's talk about your book," I said.

She blushed and covered her face with both hands. I laughed.

"Do we have to?" she murmured.

"Yes. We need to get comfortable talking to each other, and the novel is neutral territory."

She dropped her hands and looked at me.

"For you, maybe."

"Fair enough. But to be honest, I've never read a book like that before. I want to talk about it. Like, is this something women are really into? All this romance and shit? I mean, isn't it enough that a guy is an animal in bed?"

She stared at me dumbly.

"Uh, no."

"Why not?"

"Because sex isn't everything. A woman wants to feel loved, appreciated, respected. Besides, you have to get to the sex, don't you?"

"I know how to get to the sex."

She sighed and rolled her eyes.

"Haven't you ever longed for anything more meaningful?"

"Nope."

I started walking again and after a moment she raced to catch up.

"What is it?" she asked. "I can tell you want to say something else."

"I do, but I don't know how to say it without hurting your feelings."

She snorted.

"I think we're past that."

"When you describe the first kiss, well, it's not great. I could tell you'd never been well-kissed."

The smile dropped from her face and she studied me. We stopped walking again and faced each other.

"So kiss me," she said.

"Excuse me?"

"For research, you know. You must be quite good at it. Kiss me and I'll know how to write about it."

The request shocked the hell out of me.

"No," I said.

"Why not?"

"Because I don't want to. Listen, I told you I'd be affectionate in front of your parents, but that's it. I'm not some research subject."

She looked out towards the water. There was one lone fishing boat out, rocking with the waves up against the horizon.

"So describe it to me," she said softly.

"Describe it to you?" I asked, dubious.

"Yes. Describe the experience of being kissed. Or of kissing someone. What do you consider the perfect kiss?"

I thought about it for a few minutes before answering her.

"Well, kisses fall into different categories. There are urgent kisses, long make-out sessions, fucking panicked kisses... Sometimes they're a pit stop, sometimes they're the final destination. But my favourite kind starts out slow, gentle. Waiting to see if you'll melt against each other before deepening the kiss. And then it kind of picks up. You get into it. You get turned on. The kiss takes on a life of its own."

I glanced over at her and she looked thoughtful, so I continued.

"I remember when I was a teenager and making out was the bomb. I knew I wasn't getting any further, so I put everything into those make-out sessions. But then you move on, you get to first base, then second, then third, and by the time you know it, you're having sex. And you mistakenly believe that each step is better than the last, so you never really go back to just making out. I'd love that, actually—to go back to just making out. Start again."

I paused for a moment, realizing I'd told her something I'd never even articulated for myself before. I checked for her reaction, but her expression was blank. I cleared my throat, sheepish grin on my face.

"That was good, uh, research. Thanks," she said.

"No problem," I said. "Listen. I've got to get back to work."

"Right. Of course."

She stood up, stumbling over the log. She had this clumsy streak that I found amusing. Almost charming. I waited until she sorted herself out, then stood up, and together we headed back into the woods.

CHAPTER FIVE
Maggie

I walked slowly back to my rented cottage, reflecting on my conversation with Liam. His description of a kiss had left me feeling unsettled. The kisses I'd experienced had been rushed, sloppy, or chaste. I had felt none of that magic he'd described, no melting. Just nervous hands, cold lips, and a firm insistence.

When I got home, there was a parcel waiting outside my door. I picked it up and carried it inside, curious, as I hadn't ordered anything recently. I opened it up and pulled out a folded note. It was from my parents: *Just sending a few advanced supplies. So we won't be a bother during our visit.*

I rifled through the package, finding bottles of meal supplements, vitamins, and two jars of my father's favourite marmalade. I closed the whole thing and shoved it under the kitchen island. I still had some time before their arrival. I didn't need constant reminders every time I opened the fridge or pantry.

I whipped up an easy dinner and sat down at my computer to start my second job. I stared at the screen, but no words would come. Discouraged, I walked to the closet and pulled out a jigsaw puzzle, setting it on the dining room table. Whenever I was blocked, it was the best way to clear my mind. And for the first time since arriving in Mountain Valley, I was blocked.

*

"So that boyfriend of yours, he's really cute. How'd you meet?"

I was standing at reception while I waited for Tammy to finish up. We had fallen into the habit of walking home together after work. She had not stopped questioning me about Liam since the moment he walked into the hotel.

Over the past two weeks, he'd come by often during his afternoon break to take a walk. I could tell she was perplexed by the whole situation, so I decided to put her out of her misery.

"My brother introduced us."

She whistled.

"That's some brother you've got. Mine would issue a restraining order against a guy like that."

I smiled.

"He's okay. Don't judge a book by its cover."

"Oh, I'm not. But it is Liam Grayson. I've done my research."

Shit.

"Okay, Tammy. Here's the deal. We're not actually dating."

"What?" She grabbed her purse before taking my elbow to guide me towards the door. "What do you mean? He's been here almost every day."

As we walked through the streets, I explained the situation to her, frankly grateful to have a friend I could confide in. She listened, fascinated, and was silent for a few minutes before responding.

"That's a pretty stupid plan. But I hope you're at least going to fuck him."

I laughed out loud.

"Not part of the agreement," I said.

"Shame."

I turned to her, considering my words carefully before speaking.

"You really think so?"

"Hell, yeah. Look at that man. He's hot, he knows his way around a kitchen, and I bet you he's a beast between the sheets."

"And that's enough for you?"

Tammy stopped walking, taking me by the shoulders and shaking me lightly.

"What is wrong with you?"

"Nothing. I just...where's the romance?"

"Ah, you're one of those. You want to be wooed and loved. Don't you see the beauty in a one-night stand? Or in your case, a six-night stand? This is like a gift, being served up to you on a silver platter."

"I'm not interested," I said.

"How is that even possible? You've seen him, right? Like, you actually look at him when you're together? Have you seen the size of his hands? Good lord, what those hands could do —"

Tammy made the hand signals for exploding bombs by the side of her head.

"Frankly, I just don't see the fuss."

"What? With him?" she asked. "He's not your type?"

"No, not with him. With sex, in general."

Tammy stopped so fast she almost fell over.

"Excuse me?"

I sighed, getting ready to explain myself once again.

"I guess I'm just not the most sexual of people. Frankly, I can't understand what you see in it."

Tammy shook her head as if she couldn't believe what she was hearing. I realized I was espousing an unpopular opinion, but I stood by it and was determined not to be ashamed of it.

"You just haven't had good sex," she said. "Get back to me when this little experiment is over."

"I told you already, that's not part of the arrangement."

"Uh, huh. Sure. Listen, this is me. You're off tomorrow, right?"

"Yeah, my folks arrive in the afternoon."

"Okay. Good luck. Keep me posted."

*

The next morning, I got up early, my stomach in knots. There was nothing left for me to do. I'd scrubbed the house from top to bottom, put fresh flowers in the guest room, and stocked the pantry full of my parents' supplements. I'd even emptied a drawer in my dresser for Liam and moved the bed aside so I'd have more space on the floor.

The bell rang at ten, and I tried to quell the

butterflies that had suddenly taken flight in my belly. I opened the door and Liam stood there, suitcase in hand, shit-eating grin on his face.

"Honey, I'm home."

He leaned down and kissed me on the cheek. That was something we hadn't practiced, and it caught me off guard. My breath hitched as I caught a whiff of his scent—some vaguely familiar aftershave and a faint hint of lemon. I backed away, flustered, and led him into the house. I heard him chuckle softly behind me.

"We'll go to the bedroom so you can put down your stuff," I said, guiding him upstairs.

My bedroom was a decent size—queen bed with two

nightstands, a long dresser, and a comfy reading chair in the corner. Usually it was covered in clothing but I'd done a thorough cleaning.

"So, um, this is it. I cleared out a drawer for you." I opened the empty drawer. "And, uh, I have a mattress under the bed, fully made up. I'll sleep on the floor."

"I'll take the floor," he mumbled.

"No, really, I don't want to put you out further."

He dropped his bag on the bed and spoke while he unpacked.

"Whatever."

Great. So much for chivalry. But then again, look who I was dealing with.

After he put away his clothes and deposited a few things in the bathroom, he made a tour of the house, opening all the drawers and closets, familiarizing himself with the surroundings. I followed him, nervously.

"It's going to be fine, Em, I promise."

"Em?"

"Yeah. That's my nickname for you."

"No one calls me Em."

"Well, now I do."

"I don't like Em. I'm not an Em. Mags is fine. Trust me."

He shook his head.

"Nope. Em."

I rolled my eyes and gritted my teeth. Six nights. I could do this for six nights. Especially if it meant my parents would finally leave me alone.

We made a quick lunch together in the kitchen so he would know where everything was when my parents arrived. He figured it would be odd if the chef wasn't cooking at home, and it would certainly raise eyebrows if he started asking where the pots and spatulas were.

He watched me chop a carrot for a while, then moved in and took the knife from my hand.

"Let me show you," he said.

"I don't need lessons, thank you very much."

"Everyone should know how to use a knife. Even a writer."

He positioned himself behind me and took my hands in his. Together we held the knife, fist on the handle, thumb on the blade, as he taught me how to properly slice the carrot. He was very close, and I found it difficult to breathe. I extricated myself from the situation and went to get a jug of water from the fridge. He just watched me, amused.

"What's the matter, Em? Thought physical contact did nothing for you?" he laughed.

"Don't flatter yourself."

CHAPTER SIX

Liam

I don't know why I enjoyed making her squirm so much. I wasn't intentionally teasing her, the situations just kept presenting themselves. In my defense, she was a very easy target.

We ate together, a salad prepared using whatever leftover ingredients she had in the fridge. She was amazed at the results.

"I would've thrown half this stuff away," she said between bites.

"Sacrilege," I said, pushing another forkful into my mouth.

To test the waters, I reached over and tousled her hair. She smiled and blushed, but didn't stiffen. More progress.

We had a little time until her parents were

due to arrive, and she was clearly nervous, so I suggested we watch Netflix to get her mind off things. We sat down to choose something and had our first argument.

Turns out she likes coming-of-age shit and has no interest in *Game of Thrones* or *Dexter*. I didn't see why I should have to compromise, given the favour I was doing her, but given how anxious she was, I wisely decided this wasn't the time to argue. She put on some sappy crap and I pulled out my phone.

"Really?" she said. "That's kind of rude."

I rolled my eyes and tucked my phone away, giving my full attention to the teenage girl suffering from cancer and the handsome boy who takes her away to meet her idol. Who turned out to be a real shmuck, in my opinion. The idol, not the handsome boy. He was kind of cool.

Before I knew what was happening, the movie took an unexpected turn and when the doorbell rang, I was actually disappointed not to see how it ended. Maggie jumped up off the couch and smoothed down her shirt.

"You look fine," I said, rising to join her.

She put out her hand, indicating I should stay put, and went to get the door. From my place in the living room, I could hear the loud greetings and passive-aggressive comments about Maggie's hair and weight. I clenched my fists and took a deep breath. I did not like what I was hearing. I was suddenly glad I was there to help her out, no matter who she was.

The voices got louder as they approached, and my first thought when the three of them walked into the room was how much she looked like her parents. Had Justin been adopted? Neither parent had Maggie's red hair, but they all had the same *look* to them. In place of Maggie's lightly-freckled skin, they both had clear complexions, but her father had the same chin, and she and her mother possessed identical sculpted cheekbones and shared those bright green eyes.

"Mom, Dad, this is Liam, my boyfriend."

I stepped forward and put out my hand to greet them. They each shook in turn, neither of them bothering to hide their surprise at my appearance.

"Liam, it's wonderful to meet you. Maggie tells us you're a chef?" her mother said, a note of disbelief in her voice.

"That's right, Mrs. Grant. At Cagney's. I made reservations for the four of you tomorrow night. Justin will be driving in to join you."

Maggie's father's face lit up at the mention of his son's name.

"That's great news," he said. "I haven't seen the boy since last Christmas. I wanted to stop there first, but Sophia insisted we come see Maggie first."

Mrs. Grant elbowed her husband in the side and he shut up, throwing me a knowing glance. I stifled a laugh and turned to Maggie, who was just standing there, dumbstruck.

"Em, why don't you give your folks a tour of the house? I'll put some coffee on," I offered.

She looked over at me, then at her parents, and then seeming to remember what was going on, she smiled and took her mother's hand.

"Come. I'll show you the guest room."

*

We spent the afternoon catching up with Maggie's parents. Being Monday, the restaurant was closed and I had a day off. They took their time looking through the cottage, checking her pantries and shit. If it had been my folks, I'd have gone apeshit at a certain point, but Maggie took it all in stride. I guess it was what she knew.

They had a bunch of questions for me, and I did my best to answer as honestly as I could. We'd obviously built a backstory that we'd both memorized, so those questions came easy. But at a certain point, Mr. Grant turned to me and said, "So what is it exactly you see in my daughter?"

"Excuse me?" I asked, certain I'd misheard him.

"Well, you're from two very different backgrounds and to be honest, I can't even imagine how you met," he said.

"It's like we told you, Dad. We were set up," Maggie interjected.

"Oh, yeah. Right. Well, anyway, I'm still curious."

I glanced over at Maggie and saw her panicked expression. Ms. Organized was freaking out that we didn't have a plan in place for this line of questioning.

"Well, for starters, she's super organized. Likes everything in its place," I started. Maggie glared at me, but I continued. "She's got it together. That's good. And it's funny how worried she gets when things don't go according to plan."

"That's why you fell in love with her?" Mrs. Grant asked, dubious.

"Well, she's pretty cute. Look at those freckles. They kill me. And she's smart as hell. We do kind of hate each other's taste in television, but that's okay."

Mr. Grant laughed and I took that as a good

sign. I looked over at Maggie—she was still looking pretty nervous—but I thought I'd done okay. Mr. Grant turned to his daughter.

"What about you? What do you see in him?"

Maggie turned to me and looked me up and down.

"Well, he's brutally honest, isn't he?"

CHAPTER SEVEN
Maggie

We sat down for dinner, squished to one side of the table due to my jigsaw puzzle. I tried a slow, silent count to ten to calm myself. Liam had prepared a salad and a pasta dish, which my parents appreciated, quite vocally, after their long drive and lack of home-cooked food. For dessert, he'd made a soufflé, a show-off move in my mind, but one that worked to impress my parents.

It amazed me how all it took was a display of his culinary talents to win them over. My father showed a renewed interest as soon as he tasted the salad, and spent the meal asking him about cooking techniques for a porterhouse steak.

"Why do you need to know that?" my

mother interjected. "You can't eat like that anymore. Liam, don't answer him."

Liam flashed me a look and I shrugged my shoulders. My father was going to eat whatever the hell he wanted, regardless of the number of supplements she shoved down his throat. I had no interest in getting involved in that old argument.

"So Mom, tell me, what kind of stuff have you seen?" I asked her, figuring I could at least provide a distraction.

"Oh, Maggie, you should see the birds. Depending on where we are, they're different, but the cardinals are my favourite."

She went on a twenty-minute ornithological tirade, most of which I blocked out as I tried to figure out what would happen after dinner. Things seemed to have gone okay so far. Maybe a little tense for a couple supposedly madly in love, but everyone had their days, right?

After dinner, Liam suggested we head to the living room while he cleaned up. I protested, but he steered me out of the kitchen. He may have just wanted some time away from my crazy family, so I joined my parents on the couch as my dad flipped through the Netflix options.

"Don't you have regular TV?" he asked.

"Nope."

"Well, what if I want to watch *Jeopardy!*?"

"So, watch *Jeopardy!* Any time you want."

His head whipped around to look at me.

"You serious?" he asked.

I nodded. He found the search screen and let out a laugh when he found *Jeopardy!* He settled into the couch and started his age-old yelling match with the TV. My mom turned to me.

"So, sweetheart, is everything okay between you and Liam?" she asked.

"Yeah. Of course. Why would you ask?"

"Because I'm a woman, and I can tell when things are a little...off," she said gently.

Shit.

"Well, you just happened to come the day after a big fight. I'm sure we'll work everything out and it'll be fine by morning."

"If you say so," she paused. "Should your father and I put in earplugs tonight?"

"MOTHER!"

*

After a few rounds of *Jeopardy!*, Liam came to join us in the living room. I thanked him profusely for doing the dishes, and he gave me weird look.

"Why would you thank me now? To look good in front of your folks? I do this every night," he said.

I swallowed, realizing my error. I cast a glance at my parents, but they were both laughing at a contestant who'd forgotten to format her answer as a question.

"Right," I said, under my breath.

He sat down on the armchair, leaving the couch to me and my parents. My mom, over my father's loud protests, reached for the remote and lowered the volume.

"That was a truly excellent dinner, Liam. Thank you. Can I ask what led you to become a chef?" she asked.

Liam smiled, almost as if to himself at some private recollection.

"I've always liked being in the kitchen, and I've always been good with my hands. It wasn't until I was a little older and more experienced that I began to realize I also had a knack for creating flavours and textures that other people really enjoyed. My parents were not supportive. Haven't spoken to them in over a decade. But I love the life. It's rock and roll, non-stop."

I listened as he peeled away the layers and I got a glimpse of the real Liam, the man behind the self-confident womanizer with the big muscles and multiple tattoos.

"That's fascinating," my mother said. "It

does sound like a true calling. But like my husband earlier, I still can't reckon how the two of you got together."

"Well," he said. "Sometimes opposites attract, don't they?"

"Okay, enough already. Can we watch TV?" my father said.

I sighed in relief, grateful for once for my father's complete lack of social skills. He was the one person in the room who wanted this conversation to end more than I did. I could've hugged him.

"What do you want to watch now, Dad?" I asked, willing to give him the moon.

"Does this thing have *Die Hard*?"

Liam reached over and grabbed the remote.

"You bet your ass it does."

He found the film within twenty seconds and I went into the kitchen to make some popcorn. Apparently, there was still family time to be had.

CHAPTER EIGHT

Liam

After the movie ended, the Grants disappeared into the guest room.

"Finally. Either they're exhausted or they've had enough of me for the day," Maggie said.

"Does it really matter which?"

"No. It does not." She paused. "Thanks. Again."

"My pleasure," I said.

She unfolded herself and got up from the couch, picking the empty mugs off the coffee table.

"I'm going to head to bed. You can watch TV or whatever. Just, um, don't worry about waking me when you come in. I go to sleep pretty late."

"So why don't you stay and watch

something with me?" I asked.

"This is kind of my writing time," she explained.

"Okay. Good to know. I'll leave you to it, then."

I watched her disappear up the stairs and then picked up the remote and flipped on the TV. What a strange fucking day. I couldn't remember the last time I'd met a girl's parents. And here I'd spent an entire afternoon entertaining the Grants, and then cooking for them, all for a woman I barely knew.

I flipped through the stand-up specials until I found something that appealed to me, then settled in to watch. But after about half an hour, I found myself growing tired. Not wanting to fall asleep on the couch and send the wrong signal to her parents come morning, I got up and headed upstairs to Maggie's bedroom.

I stood outside the door for a few seconds, wondering if I should knock or just go right in. What did people who lived together do? Did they just walk in? That would be kind of rude. What if it were me, and I was rubbing one out?

I knocked gently.

"Come in," Maggie called.

I opened the door and found her sitting cross-legged on the armchair, computer on her lap, typing away. She was wearing a white T-shirt and thin grey cotton shorts. Her hair was all tied up on the top of her head in a messy… something or other. But the thing that really got me was her glasses. She was wearing a pair of round, tortoise-shell frames that made her look sexy as hell. And much to my horror, for the first time since this entire charade began, my dick stood up and took notice of the situation.

Suddenly, I was no longer doing a favour for my friend's kid sister. I was in a bedroom, preparing to spend the night, with an incredibly hot woman. I grabbed some clothes and made a beeline for the bathroom.

I walked in, closed the door, and turned on the cold water. I splashed my face and looked in the mirror. *Get a fucking grip, man.* What the hell had just happened? I got ready for bed, brushed my teeth, and walked back into the bedroom. She glanced up at me and smiled and once again, I felt that stirring in my shorts. I walked over to the laundry hamper to drop my clothes in, then leaned over to pull the mattress out from under the bed.

"How's the writing going?" I asked, trying to break the tension.

"Um, okay," she said. "I rewrote a bunch after our walk the other day. Want to take a look?"

She uncrossed her legs and stood up, handing me the laptop. I took it from her and sat down on the edge of the bed. She paced as I read. It was clear from the revisions she'd made that she had been listening when I'd described the kiss, but it was also still clear she'd never experienced a proper one. I handed her back the laptop.

"It's getting there," I said.

She looked at me, frustration clouding her face.

"But I wrote it just like you described. What's wrong now?" she demanded.

"You wrote it just like *I* described. You need to find your own words, your own description."

"Well how the fuck am I supposed to do that?" she asked.

"Get yourself kissed."

"You're supposed to be my boyfriend. Kiss me."

I laughed.

"We've been over this already—"

"Right. My brother. You don't like me. You have a million different reasons. But I'm a grown woman and—newsflash—my brother's not my keeper. And I'm sure you've kissed hundreds of women you didn't like."

She was standing there, hands on her hips, looking incredibly pissed off. I set the laptop down on the bed and stood up.

"And what's so funny, anyway? You've had this stupid grin on your face since you walked in here. Like this whole situation is hysterical. Like it's just *beyond* that I'd ask you—"

I grabbed her head in my hands and kissed her. Partly just to shut her up, partly because of those damn glasses, but mostly because I'd suddenly noticed the way her mouth moved when she spoke, how her lips curled up at the corner.

My intention had been a short kiss, just a small demonstration. But then it happened— the melt. I stood there, stunned, as her lips parted and her arms came up around my neck. I moved one hand to the back of her head, shifting the angle of my mouth to deepen the kiss.

My blood turned to fire and I could not get enough of her. She broke away for air and I bent my head, kissing the hollow of her neck. A low sigh escaped her lips and I covered her mouth with mine once more. She pressed herself up against me, tentatively, and I felt myself grow hard.

I pulled back and cleared my throat.

"So, uh. There you have it. A proper kiss."

She stood there, blinking at me.

"I'm just going to run down to the kitchen and get some water. You want anything?"

She shook her head slowly, running her thumb over her bottom lip, still not saying a word. I backed away from her, turned the knob, and slipped out of the room.

CHAPTER NINE

Maggie

That was a kiss?

I sat down on the edge of the bed and stared at the closed door. My heart was racing and I was finding it difficult to breathe. I crawled under the covers and turned off the bedside light, staring at the ceiling and wondering if I should fake sleep when Liam got back.

In a million years, I'd never expected him to kiss me. In a million years, I never thought I'd like it. But I had liked it. A lot. He'd been so right in his description about the melting together. I had never experienced that before. And when he traced the bottom of my lip with his tongue? Holy shit. My belly did a little flip at the memory, and I slid my hand under the covers, reaching down between my legs, surprised to find myself damp. I pushed aside my panties and slid one finger across my opening, so slick and ready.

I shifted a little, careful not to make any noise as I ran my thumb lightly over my clitoris, arching my back at the unexpected pleasure that coursed through me. I swallowed and glanced at the door, eyes wide open but my head filled with images of Liam towering over me, his hands in my hair, his tongue in my mouth.

The door burst open and light poured into the room. I pulled my hand out from between my legs and rolled over onto my side, hoping he hadn't seen anything. He quietly closed the door and made his way to the makeshift bed on the floor, noisily adjusting the covers and fluffing the pillows. I closed my eyes, torn between trying to ignore the dull ache between my legs and wishing he'd go to sleep so I could finish what I'd started.

*

The next morning, Liam was gone by the time I woke up. There was a note on the bedside table: *Had to open today. See you at dinner.* I said a silent prayer of thanks that I didn't have to face him first thing in the morning. And then I threw in an extra prayer, asking that this be his schedule for the week.

I got up, showered, and went downstairs to make breakfast for my parents. I found them already seated at the table, their home-brought newspapers unfolded before them, and their home-sent breakfast supplements half-finished.

"Oh, sweetheart. We didn't wait because we didn't know what time you'd be up," my mother said.

I forced a smile and went over to the coffee machine. I was pretty sure it must've been Liam who made the coffee. That kind of consideration wasn't my parents' style. I poured myself a cup and joined them at the table.

"I do have to work, you know," I said.

"Do you? Oh, that's a pity. We hoped you'd take the week off," my mother said.

"Sorry. Can't do it. It's tourist season. The hotel is busy."

"You wouldn't need the hotel if you got a real job," my father interjected.

"Daddy. I don't want to start this again. I'm writing a book. I don't want any other kind of job."

"Where's Liam?" my mother asked.

"He left for work. He opens the restaurant on Tuesdays. We'll see him at dinner."

"He's quite something," my father muttered.

"I will take that as a compliment. Because I'm sure you've looked past the tattoos and the salty language and found that he's a decent human being."

I got up, grabbed my bag, and stormed out of the house.

*

I was stocking the hospitality cart with folded towels when Tammy came to find me on her break.

"Hey, girl," she said, sidling up beside me. "How's the fauxmance going?"

I laughed.

"So far, so good. My parents seem to buying it."

"Have you fucked him yet?"

I turned to her, trying my best to look indignant.

"No, I have not. I told you, that's not part of the deal."

Tammy just shook her head.

"Nope. I'm sorry. There is no way that man is spending a week in your bedroom and you're not fucking him. You just tell me when it happens."

She walked away, towards the elevators, and

I called out after her, "Never going to happen."

While I was confident in that proclamation, I had to admit I'd been thinking about that kiss all day. I picked up my phone to text him a million times, but what was I going to say? *Hey, great kiss?* He'd kissed hundreds of women, I was pretty sure ours hadn't exactly been a stand-out for him.

I rolled the cart back into place and took the stairs to the locker room. After changing out of my uniform, I headed home to meet my parents and get ready for dinner.

*

We met Justin at the restaurant and there was a whole scene as my parents fussed over him, the golden child. He shot me an apologetic look, but it wasn't his fault. As the firstborn son, thirteen years my senior, he could do no wrong. I'd spent my whole life being measured against his accomplishments but had nevertheless managed to carve out a relationship of my own with my parents. It wasn't perfect, but it was something we were all able to live with. Most of the time.

Jen greeted us at the door and showed us to the best table in the house. Adam, the owner, came over to say hello and meet my parents.

He and Justin had met when Adam hired my brother's sous-chef, Toni, for Cagney's. There were no hard feelings, though, so the drinks flowed freely.

My dad and Justin spent most of the meal catching up, talking sports and politics. I tried to keep to myself, well-aware this was one of the week's rare times I wasn't the focus of my parents' interrogations.

"The food is quite good," my mother commented.

"Liam is the best chef in the area," Justin said. "Mags here landed a good one."

"He does seem interesting," my father agreed.

After dessert was served, Liam came out of the kitchen to say hello. My parents complimented him on the meal and he was equally courteous with them. He and Justin talked shop for a few minutes, and then he stood up to go.

"I'm sorry I can't stay longer. Duty calls. And Toni's off tonight, so I've got to close. I won't be home until late."

He directed that last part to me, and I nodded like the dutiful girlfriend. We had not exchanged one word since the kiss, and I was struggling to remain casual. He leaned over to kiss me goodbye, and I offered him my cheek.

But he took my chin in his hand and turned my head to face his, then kissed me softly on the mouth before walking away.

Justin stepped on my foot under the table, hard.

"Ow!" I said.

Everyone turned to look at me, except for Liam. He looked directly at Justin, catching his eye. Justin shot him a warning look, and Liam grinned, turning to walk away. We all watched as he made his way to the kitchen, stopping several times to greet guests as he weaved his way through the tables. I couldn't take my eyes off his ass. How had I never noticed it before?

"Maggie? Maggie? Did you hear me?" my mother asked.

I hadn't heard a word she said.

*

As we left the restaurant, Justin pulled me aside.

"What the hell was that?" he hissed in my ear.

"That was my boyfriend giving me a kiss goodbye," I said.

"On the mouth?" he said, incredulous.

"Hey. Liam was *your* idea. Don't throw this in my face. You knew who he was when you suggested this."

Justin stared at me as our parents walked ahead.

"Did you sleep with that motherfucker?"

"NO! Not that it's any of your business. But no. We are putting on a show for Mommy and Daddy. That's it. Just leave it."

We started walking, not really trying to catch up but eager to keep our parents in view. Justin had parked outside the restaurant, but clearly wasn't going anywhere until he was satisfied his baby sister was safe.

"Shit. I guess I really didn't think this through," he mumbled.

"Justin. I'm not interested in him. He is not my type. You've known me my whole life, you know this. Stop worrying."

"You don't understand guys like this. They have a way about them. Just do me a favour. Promise me you won't believe a damn thing that comes out of his mouth."

"Seriously?" I said.

"Yes. Seriously. Just promise me, Mags. Don't get mixed up with him."

"Okay," I said. "Okay."

CHAPTER TEN

Liam

It was close to eleven when I got home from the restaurant, and I found Maggie's father on the couch, half-asleep, watching TV. My plan to accidentally fall asleep on the couch and avoid confronting that kiss for a little while longer was shot to hell.

"Hey, that's not so bad. When you said late, I was picturing long after midnight," Mr. Grant said.

"Well, benefits of a small town. Things close down relatively early. At least during the week. I hope you enjoyed your meal."

"It was great. Really. Nice job."

I smiled my thanks and walked through towards the stairs. I went up slowly so as not to make too much noise. With any luck, she'd be asleep. I eased open the bedroom door and the lights were off, the room quiet. I breathed a sigh of relief and went in, grabbing a shirt and heading for the bathroom.

When I came out, I saw the mattress had already been pulled out. I noticed the first night when she got into her own bed she'd decided not to fight me on the sleeping arrangements. I got in and pulled up the sheet, staring at the ceiling and wondering how to handle this situation.

That kiss had been more than I'd expected. Bluntly, it had knocked me off my feet. I was finding it hard to even look at Maggie without wanting to touch her. It killed me to think that she disliked the idea of sex. That someone, or more than one someone, had so completely fucked it up with her that she actually thought she was better off without it. She'd been so damn responsive to that kiss I knew I could prove her wrong. And I had only five days left to do it.

I had a moment of moral contemplation. She was innocent. I was not. Could I really get involved with this woman for five nights without worrying she'd read something more into it? She, of the 'oh, I want a romantic love' mentality?

"Em," I whispered. "You up?"

It was quiet for so long I figured she was asleep.

"Yeah, I'm up."

"Can I ask you something?"

"Go ahead."

"Have you ever had an orgasm?"

I heard the blankets rustle as she sat up in bed.

"What?"

"You heard me. Have you ever had an orgasm?"

"Well, of course. What kind of question is that?" she demanded.

"So, you're saying another human being made you come, and you didn't enjoy it?"

There was a long pause.

"I said I'd had an orgasm. But only the self-inflicted kind."

I laughed out loud and sat up, looking for her in the dark.

"Jesus Christ. Self-inflicted? You make it sound like a wound to avoid at all costs."

"Well, you know what I mean," she said.

"I suppose. So you do masturbate?"

"Liam, I don't like you enough to get into this line of questioning."

"Research. Answer the question."

I heard an exasperated sigh and smiled to myself.

"Yes, I masturbate."

"And you enjoy it?"

"I do."

"So what makes you think that you wouldn't enjoy the same activity with a partner?"

"Why won't you let this go?" There was almost a pleading tone to her voice.

"Because I think you're a great writer. And you could be a great romance writer. You just need to spice it up a bit."

"That's what I need. A man telling me how to write romance books that other women will read."

"Fuck, Maggie, that's not what I meant."

"Anyway, it's irrelevant. I've never been with a man that's touched me the way I touch myself."

My dick sprang to attention. I tried to swallow over the lump that had suddenly appeared in my throat. I was grateful for the darkness.

"Why don't you show me?" I asked, trying my best to sound casual.

"Excuse me?"

"If you show me how you like to be touched, I bet I can make you come. And it will be just as good, if not better, than what you can pull off on your own."

"No. That's ridiculous."

"Don't be so quick to turn me down. Think about it. I'm offering you a no-strings-attached orgasm. In a few days, you'll never have to see me again. Imagine what it could do for your writing."

She didn't say another word, so I lay back down and stared up at the ceiling, waiting for her to fall asleep.

*

When I woke up the next morning, I could hear Maggie in the shower. We had still not been alone together, face-to-face in daylight hours, since the kiss. I contemplated slipping out of the room but decided not to be such a fucking coward. Two nights were already gone, I had four to go. If I was going to get anywhere with her, it was time to man up.

I got up and pushed the mattress back under the bed. I pulled on a pair of shorts but no T-shirt. I knew my assets. I made the bed for her, then sat down to wait for my turn in the shower.

She came out a few minutes later, wrapped in a terry robe, hair up in a towel. There was nothing between her and me but the soft white belt looped around her waist. One tug—

"You need the shower?" she asked.

I snapped out of it and stood up, grabbing my clothes and heading into the bathroom.

"What's your schedule?" I asked.

"I've got to be at the hotel in an hour. You?"

"Restaurant at noon. Toni's doing the prep this morning."

"Okay. I'll go down and start the coffee, we'll put on a little show for my folks, then go our separate ways?"

"Sounds good."

"You working tonight?" she asked.

"Just through dinner. I should be back by eight."

*

When I got down to the kitchen, the Grants were seated around the table, eating their breakfast and discussing plans for the day. Maggie was at the counter, buttering some toast. I walked up behind her, wrapped an arm around her waist, and kissed her behind the ear.

"Good morning," I whispered.

I saw the goosebumps rise along the back of her neck and smiled to myself. I ran my hand up her back, squeezing her shoulder before going to grab a cup of coffee. She shot me a little side-eye, but I ignored her, chuckling to myself. While in the shower, I'd devised my plan. I had made my offer, and she'd shot me down. Now it was time for her to come to me. And I had no qualms about playing dirty.

I opened the overhead cabinet and reached up for a mug, flexing my bicep in the process. They said women had tools at their disposal? So did men. I learned that secret a long time ago. I filled my cup and joined the Grants at the table, reaching for a bagel and taking a bite.

"So? Hiking? Is that what I'm hearing?" I asked, chipper as fuck.

"That's the plan. Maggie tells us there's a flat trail around somewhere?" Mr. Grant said.

"Yup. Leads right to the beach. Perfect for a day like today. Bring your swimsuits and you can cool off when you're done. Just be warned —the lake is freezing this early in the season."

"Oh, I don't think we'll be swimming," Mrs. Grant laughed.

I looked at her appraisingly.

"Come on, Mrs. G. You must look smoking in a bathing suit."

She blushed and buried her face in her newspaper. Her husband looked at her, studying her as if seeing her for the first time. Finished creating her toast Picasso, Maggie grabbed her plate and walked over to the table. Before she could get to her seat, I reached out and pulled her onto my lap. A surprised look flashed across her face, but she recovered quickly and settled in, taking a bite of her toast.

Her father glanced over his newspaper, gave me a quick look, then turned back to his news. Her mother was going on about some particular birds she was hoping to see on the trail. I was occupying myself with Maggie's freshly-shampooed hair. She smelled fabulous.

I put down my coffee cup and casually placed my hand on her leg. She stiffened but kept eating her breakfast, trying her damnedest to ignore me. She couldn't fool me. I could feel her pulse quickening through her back, against my chest. I wrapped the arm around her waist a little tighter, drawing her even closer. Then I let that other hand trail up her thigh.

She took a sharp breath in, then shifted in my lap. *Bingo.* She casually put down her toast and placed her hand on top of mine, firmly pressing down to stop me from progressing any further north. I leaned forward and whispered in her ear, "The things I could do —"

She shot up, causing the cutlery by her plate to fall to the ground. The loud noise caused both her parents to look up.

"What is it, dear?" her mother asked.

"I just realized I'm late for work. I'll see you

all later. Mom, Dad, have a great afternoon. We'll meet up here for dinner. Liam? You'll be in later tonight?"

I gave her a salute and a smile and she turned to the door.

"Don't I get a goodbye kiss?" I asked, mischievous as hell.

She flashed me a look that would've left me cold if I hadn't been running so damn hot. She walked back over and bent down gingerly, planting a soft kiss on my lips. I grabbed the back of her head, not letting her pull away until I got confirmation that the first kiss hadn't been a fluke.

It hadn't.

She pulled away, swallowing as she looked me in the eye.

"I'll, uh, see you later."

CHAPTER ELEVEN
Maggie

I was a mess at work. Completely off my game. I walked right into one room while a couple was still fast asleep. In another room, I replaced all the body wash with conditioner. By lunch, I felt like a walking zombie. All I could think about was sitting in Liam's lap, his hand moving on my thigh, the dull ache between my legs.

I thought back to all my girlfriends back home, how they'd been all boy-crazy and talked about sex. I had honestly thought they were making it all up, trying to fit in and be cool. But now, I was experiencing it, too. Decidedly late, at twenty-seven years old, but I was definitely feeling it.

What if he could make me feel good? What if

that kiss was only the beginning? I had no intention of getting emotionally involved with him, but there were certain facts on the ground to be considered: He was hot, he was willing, he was experienced, and he was sleeping in my bedroom for the next four nights.

Four nights. I could have four nights with him and that would probably be enough to equip me for ten books. I looked up from my sandwich and for the first time, noticed Tammy sitting across the table from me in the break room. She had a knowing smirk on her face.

"Don't say it," I said.

"I'm not saying anything. You'll tell me, right?"

She took a bite of her sandwich and watched me, refusing to let me escape the question.

"Would it be so terrible if I did it?" I asked.

"HELL NO!" she said, slapping her sandwich down on her plate. "Has the opportunity arose?"

I shrugged my shoulders.

"He is Liam Grayson. You said it yourself."

Tammy shivered, a pleasant smile on her face.

"Four nights with Chef Liam. Man, I'd let him make a meal of me."

"TAMMY!"

"I'm serious, Mags. This is a golden

opportunity. Just don't fall for him."

"Like I'd ever." I was silent a moment. "But why do you say that?"

She looked at me.

"And you don't think he'd ever change?" I said.

"Not a chance. That man will say anything to get into your pants. Know that before you get involved. Besides, you don't want him. I'm probably the only other woman in town who hasn't slept with him. Use him like everyone else does. He seems to enjoy it."

It sounded wrong, but everything Liam had demonstrated proved her words right. He had literally offered himself up to me, a no-strings orgasm machine. I was insane to turn him down. And there was zero risk. He wasn't my type; there was no way I'd fall for him.

Shocked at how one kiss had completely turned my life around, I walked home going over all the possible scenarios. Liam had been right about me. I liked having a plan. And so long as I stuck to the plan, everything would be fine.

*

"Honey! You're home! Did you have a good day at work?"

I was in the kitchen, prepping dinner, when my parents came in from their day. As I chopped and sauteed, my father told me about the hike while my mother interjected with little tidbits of information on each of the birds she'd spotted.

We sat down to eat and I managed to get through the meal without having to say more than the occasional yes, no, and pass the rice. My mother insisted on cleaning up and my father and I retired to the living room to find an old movie to watch. He chose *Guys and Dolls*, a favourite in our family. We loved musicals, and this one was at the top of our list.

We were about halfway through when I heard Liam come in. He greeted my parents, even kissing my mother on the cheek, before finding a place for himself beside me on the couch.

"What are we watching?" he asked.

"*Guys and Dolls,*" I answered quietly.

"Never seen it. What's it about?"

I stared at him. He'd never seen it? Who had never seen it?

"Missionary girl falls for no-good gambler?" I said, my voice dripping with disbelief.

"Missionary?" he snickered. "I don't do missionary."

I rolled my eyes as my dad let out a

sympathetic chuckle.

"Grow up," I said.

He shrugged and threw an arm over my shoulder, drawing me in close to his side.

"Whatever."

I had seen this movie hundreds of times, but for the life of me, I couldn't tell you what happened after Liam sat down beside me. For the duration of the film, his hands were somewhere on my body. Stroking my hair, rubbing my back, doing that crazy thing with his fingertips on my thigh. It was distracting, to say the least.

When the final scene played, I jumped up off the couch and announced my intention to go to bed.

"Already?" my mother asked. "It's still early."

"Yeah, well, it was a rough day at work today. I'm just going to crash."

I kissed my parents goodnight, pretending I didn't see Liam reach for me and narrowly evading his grip. As I hit the stairs, I heard my dad asking him about the proper way to grill a steak.

*

Teeth brushed, face washed, I climbed into bed

and turned out the light. I couldn't get the image of Liam out of my head. The feel of his hand on my thigh, his breath on the back of my neck.

The door opened and he walked in. He made his way quietly across the room and into the bathroom. When he came out, he got settled on the mattress. I turned his offer over in my mind one final time, weighing the pros and cons. We had four nights left. There was zero emotional connection between us. It was the perfect arrangement. And it definitely counted as research.

"Liam?" I whispered.

"Yeah?"

"Okay."

I heard the blankets shift as he sat up.

"Okay, what?"

"Okay, you can watch."

"Holy shit," he muttered under his breath. He got up and sat down on the edge of the bed. "You sure about this?"

"It's just research, right? You're telling me there's a way for me to enjoy sex. I don't believe you. If you change my mind, it might do something for my writing. There's only one way to find out, though."

I pulled the covers and aside and he slid into bed beside me. I went to pull the covers up and he stopped me. Understanding his intention, I pushed them further aside.

"I'm not quite sure how to do this," I said.

"Just relax," he said.

He rolled over and rummaged around on my night table until I heard a match strike and saw the flame from the candle I kept there.

"Oh, great. Light. That'll make it easier," I said.

"Relax. It's candlelight. I need to be able to see something, don't I? There's not even enough light here for me to see if the carpet matches the drapes."

I raised my eyebrow at him and he laughed, reaching over to tousle my hair.

"Where'd you get the glasses, Em?" he asked.

"I only wear them when I work at the computer."

"They're sexy as fuck."

I squirmed, both at the mention of fuck and the idea of him finding me sexy. Emboldened, I reached down and slid off my panties. I heard his breath catch and he rolled onto his side, propping himself up on his elbow to watch me. I risked a quick glance at his face, then quickly turned away. This would be much easier if I closed my eyes.

So I did. And the first thing I saw was his

face leaning in to kiss me, his hands exploring my body. I ran my hand up my inner thigh, like he had done earlier in the evening, and arched my back slightly as I traced the slippery wetness between my legs.

"Fuck," he murmured.

"Shh. This will be easier if I pretend you're not here."

I heard him swallow, still refusing to open my eyes. I slid one finger inside, stroking myself slowly, moving my hips as I found a rhythm. Using my thumb, I rubbed small circles around my clit, feeling my breath quicken as the tension built.

He was breathing heavily beside me and it was getting impossible to ignore his presence. I opened my eyes and turned to look at him. He was staring at me with a look of pure hunger, his eyes fixed on me like I was the last meal on earth. I arched my back again, bringing myself closer to the edge, and he reached down and pulled my hand away.

"Stop," he said, his voice thick and husky. "I get the picture."

He put my hand aside, and then ever so slowly, ran his hand up my thigh, between my legs, until his thumb found my clit, repeating the same actions I'd demonstrated seconds earlier. I moaned, unable to contain myself, and reached over to grab hold of the back of his head.

He looked down at me, watching my expression, gauging my reaction to his every touch. He was going off-script, but it was all good.

"Em—" He looked down towards my breast, then back up at me.

"You want to touch me there?" I asked. He nodded. "That wasn't part of the deal."

"Maybe not explicitly, but I said I could make it as good, or even better. Let me make it better."

I considered this, then raised my shirt up above my breasts. He removed his hand from between my legs and I instantly regretted this course of action. But when his finger skimmed across my nipple, I had to bite my lip in order not to cry out.

"So you like breast play. Noted."

I hadn't known that.

He dipped his head and took one nipple in his mouth, causing minor explosions in my brain. The feeling was so intense, I felt it between my legs. I took his hand, guiding it back down, needing him to touch me there again.

Without releasing my nipple, he slipped two fingers inside me, the dual sensation causing me to moan so loud I reached for a pillow to cover my face. Then he pinched my clit. Lightly at first, then insistently. I bucked my hips, and he started to move his thumb in a circular motion, pressing down while his fingers worked inside me.

It was all too much. I had never felt anything like this before in my life. This was *not* the way it had been with other guys. They had been focused on themselves, their own pleasure. This was all about me. His hands were everywhere, his mouth firmly attached to my breast. My legs started shaking and I knew I was close. There had been no slow build, no clear warning, just a sudden, overpowering orgasm that coursed through my body, leaving me positively shattered in its wake.

Liam ran his tongue one last time around my nipple before pulling his hand out from between my legs. I lay there, paralyzed, trying to catch my breath, wondering what the fuck had just happened. I'd had orgasms. Many orgasms. And they'd all been exactly the way I wanted them because I'd been the one controlling them.

But this? This was completely different. I turned to him.

"So, it's got something to do with relinquishing control, right?"

He smiled and got out of the bed, making himself comfortable on the floor before answering.

"Now you got it."

CHAPTER TWELVE

Liam

It was hands-down the most beautiful orgasm I'd ever seen. So beautiful I couldn't get it out of my mind all day. Twice Toni came over to check on me, as I'd been over-prepping the entire morning. She threw a soup on the menu at the last minute to get rid of all the vegetables I'd cut up.

"You barely even do prep anymore. What's gotten into you?" she asked.

Adam walked into the kitchen just then.

"What's up, boss?" I asked.

"I was just coming in to tell you we've got a couple of VIPs tonight, but frankly I'm more interested in this discussion. What is going on?"

"What do you mean? Both of you?

Everything is fine," I insisted.

"I don't know," Adam mused. "I think it's got something to do with this showmance you've got going on."

"Meaning?"

"Meaning I've seen you walking around with that look on your face. I've met Justin's sister. You're too good for her. Don't do anything stupid," he said.

"For Christ's sake. Can we leave this alone?"

The two traitors exchanged knowing glances and left me to my work. Adam discussed the VIPs in hushed tones with Toni, and I plugged in my headphones and got back to chopping celery.

*

At around five o'clock, Maggie sent a text letting me know she was having a late dinner with her parents at a French restaurant down the street and asking if I'd come by when I was done my shift so we could all walk home together. I sent her a thumbs up.

I spent the next several hours in the weeds, cooking up a storm with Toni and seeing lots of empty plates coming back. It was my kind of night. Bree came into the kitchen with cocktails and we toasted a great service. As I was packing up my knives, Toni came over and waited silently by my side.

"Yes?" I asked.

"Going to see your fake girlfriend?" she asked.

"Yes, I am."

"You're sure there's nothing...?"

She let the question trail off, and I waited. She just stared at me.

"Toni. There's nothing going on. I owe Justin, you know that. It's just a few more days. Once her parents are gone, we're done. There is nothing between us."

"I don't know, Chef. Seems like she's messing with your head."

*

When I got to the restaurant, the Grants had just finished eating and were lingering over coffee and dessert. I said a quick hello, then went over to see Jerome, the owner, and took care of the bill. In a small town, it was essential to build relationships.

My phone rang as I was walking back to the table. I glanced at the Caller ID, nervous it would be some woman I'd made plans with and had forgotten about, but it was Duke, my contractor.

"Duke, what's up?"

"Liam. Sorry, man. I know it's late. I just knew you'd want to know as soon as we were done. We're done. You can move back in tomorrow," Duke said.

"Wow. That was fast. Fantastic. Send me the invoice."

I hung up the phone and sat down to join them at the table. Maggie eyed me curiously, and I shook my head slightly, indicating we shouldn't discuss it at the moment. She took the hint and turned to her mother.

"So? We ready? We can walk back home through the square. It's such a nice night, and there's usually a band playing during the summer," she said.

"Sounds lovely. Let's do it." Mrs. Grant stood up and waited for her husband to join her. I got up and put out my hand for Maggie. She took it, getting to her feet, and then didn't let go as we walked out the front door.

"Darn, the bill," Mr. Grant grunted.

"Taken care of," Jerome called from the back of the restaurant.

The Grants all turned to me and I shrugged, sheepish. Mrs. Grant leaned in towards her daughter and said in a whisper I wasn't meant to hear, "He's all right."

When we got outside, the warm air hit us

like a wall after the air conditioning of the restaurant. It was unusually hot for June, but I had no complaints. We'd come out of a long, cold winter and I loved summer in Mountain Valley. This would be my second one, and if last year had been any indication of the number of incredible women who passed through over the course of three months... I glanced down at Maggie, but it wasn't like she could read my mind or anything.

It was close to nine, but still light out. There were tons of people around—families with young children, elderly couples, young lovers —the sleepy little town had come alive. Sure enough, there was music coming from the square, and we crossed the street and made our way over, Maggie and I staying a few paces behind her parents.

"So how was your day?" she asked.

"It was great. Busy. You?"

"It was okay. I was, uh, kind of distracted."

I looked down at her and grinned, squeezing her hand.

"We've got three more nights. Let's see how much more damage, I mean research, we can do."

"What did you have in mind?" she asked, lowering her voice despite the noise of the crowd.

I stopped walking and turned to face her, leaning down and whispering in her ear.

"Has anyone ever gone down on you before?"

I watched in delight as the blush crept up her neck, colouring her cheeks and making her freckles all but vanish.

"I'll take that as a no. Well, then. If you thought last night was something—"

"Liam!"

"I've been told I'm quite good at it, actually."

"LIAM!"

Her parents turned to look at us, her mother shooting a questioning look. Maggie smirked in return, then turned back to me with a mortified expression.

"Stop it," she pleaded.

"Research, Em, remember? Research."

CHAPTER THIRTEEN

Maggie

My father headed straight for the living room when we got home, picking up the remote and settling into the couch.

"Whose turn to pick tonight? Liam?"

Liam kicked off his shoes and followed my father into the living room.

"Why don't we do something else tonight? Ever play poker?"

"You know, I always wanted to learn, but the missus never let me."

"Perfect. I'll teach you."

Liam walked over to the junk drawer and pulled out a deck of cards. I was impressed he'd remembered that. My mother walked over and stood beside me.

"I don't like this," she whispered.

"Oh, come on, Mom. Daddy is a grown man. You can't micromanage him. Wouldn't you rather he learn a new skill?" I asked.

She sighed and went into the living room. It was her habit to ignore the things she couldn't control. I, on the other hand, was fascinated.

"You play?" I asked Liam.

He shot me a look.

"Of course I play. Where else do you think I am every Sunday night?" he asked, adding. "You hit your head or something?"

My father was so enthralled by the idea of learning how to play poker that he didn't even notice my blunder. I raised my eyebrows at Liam and he shrugged, turning his attention back to my dad.

"Where did you learn to play?" my father asked him. "Is this some chef thing?"

"No, not really. I met this guy in the States one year. A real heavy metal dude who was on tour. Sat next to him at a poker table and he was the most incredible player I'd ever seen. Told him I'd cook a private dinner for him and the band one night if he taught me how to play. Now *that* was a night to remember," he said wistfully.

"Perfect," I said. "I'm going to go write for a bit."

I was eager to make my escape, not able to

cope with the idea of another night of being tormented by Liam in front of my parents. Liam shot me a look, but I ignored him. He'd clearly wormed his way into my parents' hearts because they made zero objection over the fact that I was abandoning them with the large, muscled, tattooed man. In fact, it almost seemed as if my father were bonding with him.

I went up to my room, got undressed, and jumped in the shower. I figured it would be a good idea to cool off a little. I wrapped my hair up in a towel, slipped on my robe, then tucked my legs up under me on the armchair and started writing. Using the past few nights as inspiration, I elaborated on my story, adding in texture and details that made it come alive on the page.

I have no idea how much time passed before Liam walked into the room. I didn't even hear him come in. It was only when he cleared his throat that I started and looked that I saw him watching me with an amused expression on his face.

"In the zone?" he asked.

"Completely," I answered, turning my attention back to the screen.

"How's it going?" he asked.

I tried to avert my eyes as he pulled off his pants and pulled on a pair of pajama bottoms.

It wasn't easy. I shifted in my chair.

"It's been going pretty well," I said.

"Yeah? Getting that real-life experience you were missing?"

I smiled behind my laptop, peering over to see him strip off his shirt. *Holy Jesus.* Did pots and pans weigh a hundred pounds each? I quickly looked back down, not wanting to get caught ogling.

"I guess you can say that," I replied. "You want to read some?"

"I've got a better idea," he said, dropping to the floor at my feet. "Why don't you read to me?"

He rested his chin on my knee, looking up at me with an irresistible expression on his face. I cleared my throat and started reading.

"He walked me home through the dark streets, close enough that I could smell the faint scent of his cologne. I glanced over at him, the sharp outline of his jaw prominent in the moonlight. The cobblestones were still wet from the rain, and I stumbled as I tried to keep pace.

He reached out, taking me by my elbow and guiding me closer towards him.

'Wouldn't want you falling,' he said.

The feel of his skin against mine was intoxicating. I gazed up at him, staring down at me with his piercing blue eyes, and felt the warmth radiate from the centre of my being. He ran his fingertip along the side of my cheek, stopping to tuck a stray curl behind my ear."

As I read, Liam's hand found its way under my robe and was making a slow path up along my thigh. I shifted in the chair.

"He leaned in, so slowly it felt like time had stopped. I closed my eyes, and when his lips touched mine, fireworks exploded in my head."

"Is that what it was like?" he murmured, dipping his head to kiss my knee.

I let out something akin to a squeak and tried to focus on my reading.

"His arms wrapped around me, pulling me in close so I felt the heat of his body. The blood in my veins turned to fire at his touch, making me bold, making me want him. I deepened the kiss, getting up on my tiptoes and clasping my hands behind his neck."

Liam had spread apart my robe, exposing me completely. He let out a low whistle.

"Shit, you are a redhead."

"His hand dropped to my waist, working its way up underneath my top, cupping my breast, testing its weight in his palm."

"Jesus Christ, look at you," he murmured, before leaning forward and burying his head between my thighs. I was already so wet from reading to him, from the anticipation of what I knew was coming. The laptop slid from my hand and I heard the soft thunk as it landed on the carpeted floor. I slid down in the chair as Liam raised my legs, resting them on his shoulders as he explored my most intimate parts with his tongue.

"Holy shit," I groaned.

He glanced up at me, grinning. I reached to take off my glasses and his hand closed around my wrist, stopping me.

"Leave them on," he commanded, shaking his head from side to side.

The stubble from the day's growth on his jaw scraped against the tender flesh of my inner thighs. I arched my back, seeking more.

"Good?" he asked.

"Stop talking."

He laughed and, using his tongue, traced a line from my opening up to my clit, which he coaxed into his mouth, sucking ever so gently. It was a sensation beyond anything I'd ever felt before, and my ass rose off the chair as I tried to keep myself from crying out.

He pulled back and blew on me gently, and an entirely new set of nerve endings awoke. He nipped at the insides of my thighs and I held his head with my hands, grasping at his short hair for traction.

"Fuck," I cried.

"You want me to stop?" he asked, still smiling.

"No!" I pushed his head back into position and with one hand he reached up to cup my breast, teasing the nipple as he worked his magic on my clit.

"Too much," I whispered, frantic.

My body was taking me places it had never been before. I was legitimately scared. I sat up in the chair, holding onto him as he relentlessly licked, nipped, sucked, and made love to me with his tongue. His hands slid under my ass, grasping me, grounding me. My hips moved involuntarily and I began to grind into him, riding his face as all rational thought left my body.

"Fuck yeah," he growled, squeezing my ass.

It was too much. I raised my head and looked down at him, face between my legs, broad shoulders flexing as his hands worked my ass. I had never seen anything so erotic in my life.

"Oh, god."

I wrapped my legs around his neck, holding on for dear life as the orgasm rushed me, taking complete control of my body. Liam's hand flew up to cover my mouth and I bit down, riding out the waves as he gently kissed the insides of my thighs. When I finally came down, I looked at him, only to find him gazing at me appreciatively.

"I gotta tell you, Em, when you come, it is truly a sight to behold."

I blushed.

"I'm just saying," he continued. "It's a real shame to deny so many men the pleasure of seeing that."

He got up on his feet and dropped a kiss on my forehead.

"I won't bother asking if you enjoyed it," he said, walking into the bathroom and turning on the shower.

CHAPTER FOURTEEN

Liam

I went by my apartment on the way to work the next morning. I hadn't gone by since the contractor called to tell me the work was complete. I walked in the front door and the first thing that struck me was the quiet. Had it always been this quiet?

I walked through the apartment, checking the plaster repairs and the bathroom reno. Satisfied, I went back to the living room and dropped down on the couch. I had half an hour before I had to be at the restaurant, and I figured I'd enjoy some alone time, something I'd been without the entire week.

But within a few minutes, I was bored. I picked up my phone and texted Maggie.

How's your day going?

I quickly got a reply.

It just started. Let me go work.

I'm bored. Entertain me.

I thought you said this arrangement was no strings attached.

Touché. Then I saw the three dots.

Where are you?

I realized I hadn't told her the apartment was ready.

I'm at my place. Reno is done. Looks great.

Great. Gotta go work. Later.

I shoved my phone back in my pocket and sat there a while longer. A few more days and my life would be mine again. I could get back to working hard and partying harder. For some reason, the thought didn't thrill me. I decided to head into work and take down a side of beef. That would clear my head.

*

I was well aware of the huddle taking place across the room as I muttered to myself while using my largest santoku knife to part meat from bone. I was standing behind a work table, my apron drenched in blood and a pile of cow parts sitting before me. Adam, Toni, and Bree were all watching me, apprehensive.

"You sure everything is okay?" Toni called.

"Positive," I grunted, hacking away through a piece of sinew.

"I've seen him like this once before, when he was after this blond who wouldn't give him the time of day," Adam said in a stage whisper to the other two. The meat separated from the bone. *Success.*

"This has nothing to do with Maggie," I said.

"You're sure?" Bree asked for the millionth time.

I put down the knife and turned to them.

"Her parents leave in two days. After that, it's done. Finished. Got it?"

I turned back to my work.

*

It was a late night at the restaurant. Toni had been gracious and covered for me most of the week so I could help Maggie out, but once Friday came around and the weekend crowds descended, I had no choice but to stay until closing.

I took advantage of the time away from Maggie to remind myself what my life was all about: the kitchen, the booze, the available women. When the last diners left and Bree started pouring staff drinks, I had no reservations about staying late and drinking my share.

I had zero desire to bump into Maggie's father in the living room, or her mother in the kitchen preparing a late-night snack, which she wouldn't fucking need if she ate properly during the day. I'd gotten in the habit of bringing leftovers home and more than once I'd caught her at the fridge, take-out box in hand, a guilty expression on her face. I wanted to scream at her, *instead of a meal supplement, eat a fucking meal.*

I realized my mood was not conducive to Maggie's cause, so I made sure it was past one when I walked through the front door. I knew I'd blown my chance of getting any play that night, but I honestly felt it was for the best. For someone who'd subsisted on one-night stands their entire life, this on-the-regular shit was freaking me out.

The house was dark, and I was drunk as fuck. I stumbled through the kitchen towards the stairs, tripping over an area rug that I'd hated from the moment I set foot in the house. It would be good to get home, back to my own shit. I conveniently pushed aside the memory of that empty feeling I'd had that morning, sitting on my couch.

I crept past the guest room and made my

way up the stairs, using the flashlight from my phone to find my way. Had there always been this many stairs? I took a break halfway up, sitting down and burying my head in my hands. *What the fuck was I doing?*

Drinking probably hadn't been the smartest decision I'd ever made, but agreeing to do this "favour" was pretty high up on that list, too. I sat on that step for a long time, trying to figure a way out of this mess. After a while, I concluded I was far too drunk for serious thought, got up, and stumbled my way up the rest of the stairs.

I pushed open the bedroom door, closed it behind me and slowly made my way through the bedroom to the bathroom. I stripped off my clothes, down to my boxer briefs, and got ready for bed. Flipping off the light, I went back into the bedroom, got down on my hands and knees, and searched for the mattress. Nowhere. I collapsed on the floor for a moment, but the rough nub of the carpet stung my cheek.

I sat up, looked around, and for the life of me couldn't remember where she kept the damn mattress. I felt around on the floor, under the bed, nothing. I contemplated my options. I could head back to the living room and sleep on the couch, but I had serious doubts about my ability to make it down the stairs. *Fuck it.* I got up and slid into the bed next to her.

I pulled up the covers quietly, hoping not to wake her. The entire room was spinning, and I closed my eyes and willed it to slow down, even just a little. I almost hit the ceiling when I felt Maggie's hand on my thigh.

"Sorry," she murmured sleepily.

"It's okay," I said, waiting for my heart to start beating again. "I'm sorry. I had a little too much to drink. Couldn't find the mattress. Want me to hit the couch?"

She slid over closer to me, draping her arm across my stomach. My muscles clenched, unprepared for this kind of contact. My dick, however, was more than happy at this sudden turn of events. Maggie made a happy little purring sound, tracing the outline of my abs with her fingertip.

"No," she said. "You can stay."

I tried to control my breathing, but her proximity was driving me insane. I was drunk, horny, and she was all drowsy, disheveled, and sexy as hell.

"I've been thinking," she said. "It doesn't seem quite fair that I've been having all the fun these past few nights."

Oh, Christ.

"Don't worry. I've been having plenty of fun," I assured her, willing my dick to behave.

"That's not what I meant," she said. "It just seems unfair that I'm the only one who's been getting off."

I turned to her in the dark.

"I've been jerking off every night in the bathroom after you fall asleep," I confessed.

She ran her finger up the inside of my thigh.

"Well that definitely doesn't seem right."

I put my hand on hers, stopping her progress.

"I am very, very drunk," I said, adding, "In case you hadn't noticed."

"You're cute drunk."

She got up on her elbow and leaned over to kiss me lightly on the mouth. I closed my eyes and let the warmth of her lips wash over me. With my hand on her neck, I rolled her over onto her back, leaning over her and taking the kiss further. We hadn't done that since that first time. The object of this exercise was to introduce her to new things, not make out with her like a high-school girlfriend. But if she was willing, I was game.

She was completely naked, obviously having planned for this. I cursed myself for staying out so late. I'd over-thought the situation and fucked up a perfectly good night.

"I want to touch you," she whispered, splaying her fingers across the back of my head as I took one of her magnificent tits in my mouth.

"Be my guest," I murmured, making small circles around her nipple with my tongue.

She arched her back, pressing my head into her as she moaned softly.

"Show me," she said. "Like I showed you."

I lifted my head, gazing at her with a slight smirk.

"I can pretty much guarantee anything you do will be just fine."

She shook her head.

"Not fair. I've never done this. Show me how to please you."

I took her chin in my hands and kissed her nose.

"Why don't we do it like this? You experiment, and I'll guide you if I think you need guidance."

"Why are you making this so hard?" she asked.

"I'm not trying to. I'm trying to make you comfortable. I think a lot of your past stems from you not having any control. I want you to have complete control."

She smiled and pulled me down for another kiss. As I teased her lips open with my tongue, I felt her hand slide down the front of my boxer briefs, her fingertips graze the head of my cock.

I almost kicked her off the bed.

"I'm sorry!" she said. "You see? I have no clue what I'm doing."

I laughed.

"Em, it feels great. I promise."

She wrapped her hand around me, stroking tentatively, and it felt fucking amazing. She leaned over slowly, shyly, and licked my nipple, which once again almost made me hit the ceiling. I couldn't recall any woman having done that to me before, and I'm pretty sure I'd have said no if they'd asked. But holy shit. I groaned, and she took that as encouragement, taking the nipple in her mouth and sucking gently like I'd done to her.

I reached down and wrapped my hand around hers, guiding her up and over the head of my cock, then back down again. She lifted her head and kissed me again, growing bold as she realized the effect she was having. I let go of her hand, running my fingertips up her side, skimming her breast as I made my way up to her mouth. I traced my thumb along her lower lip, and she opened her mouth, drawing my thumb inside gently with her teeth.

The combined feeling of her hand wrapped around my cock and her mouth wrapped around my thumb was driving me fucking crazy. Endurance was a source of pride with me, but I didn't think I was going to last another minute like this. From a fucking handjob.

She raised her head and kissed me again, with so much passion I couldn't believe this was the same woman I'd moved in with five days earlier. She pulled away, bit my earlobe, then whispered, "I want to taste you."

"Fucking hell," I groaned, as she slid down the bed and licked the head of my cock with the tip of her tongue.

I grabbed the sheets, not wanting to freak her out by grabbing her head, but fuck did it take restraint. I wanted nothing more than to fuck that beautiful mouth, but I lay still, letting her explore and experiment. She was clearly new at this, but she was also mightily invested.

Her warm, wet mouth sent me into another dimension. She lightly cupped my balls, running her finger along the base of my cock as she pulled me into her mouth. She tried everything—sucking, licking, a light scraping of the teeth. I clutched the sheets tighter, trying not to blow in her mouth.

When she started moaning, I completely lost it. It was one thing to have her doing this for research, it was totally another to know she was fucking enjoying it. There was nothing hotter than a woman who loved giving head.

She got up on all fours, her ass high as she ground against thin air. I slipped a hand between her legs, finding her so fucking wet I growled.

I slipped one finger inside her as my thumb worked her clit. She pumped my hand, and before long I could feel her tensing up. The woman who hated sex was mastering the art of coming rather quickly. She moaned around my cock, making me swell further in her mouth. She gripped the base, sliding her hand up and down in unison with her mouth.

She let out a cry as she came on my hand, her mouth still wrapped around my cock. It was so fucking hot I knew I was going to follow suit at any second. I grabbed her hair, pulling her away from me, not wanting to come in her mouth on her first time out.

"What the—?" she cried.

I took myself in hand, fisting my cock until I came all over her tits. She looked down, awed, and slowly reached up, rubbing my semen into her breasts. *Fuck.* Who was this woman? I closed my eyes and passed out.

CHAPTER FIFTEEN
Maggie

When I woke up on Saturday morning, Liam wasn't in bed and I didn't hear the shower running. I knew he had a later start this morning, so I figured he was downstairs having breakfast with my parents.

I rolled onto my back, stretched, and smiled at the ceiling. I had one thought on my mind. *Tonight, I get laid.*

Just the thought of it sent a thrill through my body as I remembered the feel of Liam's hands between my legs the night before. I shivered, then got up and pulled on some pajamas. I didn't have to be in until noon, so I had plenty of time to shower and get changed after eating.

Before leaving my room, I pulled the mattress from its hiding place in the closet and replaced it under the bed. Sometimes, a woman had to do what a woman had to do.

*

The smell of frying bacon hit me as I exited my bedroom. I followed the trail to the kitchen and grinned as I saw my parents at the table, Liam by the stove. I walked over to him, wrapped my arms around his waist and kissed the back of his neck.

"Good morning," I murmured.

He turned his head and gave me a proper kiss. My father cleared his throat and I pulled back, only mildly embarrassed. The whole point had been to put on a show for them. Clearly, it was working. When I glanced at my parents, they both had their noses buried in the paper, amused grins playing on their faces.

"Good morning," I said.

My father lifted his coffee cup in reply. My mom just smiled. I turned back to Liam, speaking in a quiet voice.

"I've been thinking about next steps," I said.

I saw the corners of his mouth lift as he flipped a pancake.

"Is that so?" he asked.

"Uh huh. Clearly, there's only one thing left for us to do—"

He planted another kiss on my lips before turning off the stove and carrying the plate of pancakes to the table. I picked up the bacon and followed him.

"I mean," I continued. "I don't know what my parents have planned for tonight, but afterwards—"

My mom finally dropped her newspaper.

"Oh, did we forget to tell you? We've had a change of plans. We're going to leave today and spend the weekend with Justin. He got some time off and invited us up. I thought I mentioned it."

It felt like my world came crashing down. I couldn't bring myself to look at Liam, not wanting him to see the expression of disappointment I knew was on my face.

"Don't look so disappointed, love. We'll swing by to see you again on our way home. Monday. Liam is even off, right?"

I nodded dumbly, still unable to come to grips with the fact that it was over. My parents were leaving. There was no reason for him to stick around. I swallowed and shook myself out of it.

"Right. We'll see you Monday. That'll be great. I'm sure Justin will appreciate the time with you."

We ate breakfast in relative silence, and

111

about halfway through, I risked a glance at Liam. He was sipping his coffee, looking out into space, an indecipherable expression on his face. After a moment, he put down his cup and stood, the sound of his chair scraping against the floor causing my dad to look up.

"I better go," he said.

I looked down at my lap. He didn't have to be at work for another two hours. He was probably just thrilled to be able to make an early escape. He came up behind me and planted a kiss on my head.

"Later?" he said, a note of uncertainty in his voice.

I smiled up at him. He turned to say goodbye to my folks, then left the house.

*

I sat patiently through the rest of breakfast with my parents, then said my goodbyes, telling them I had to get to work. I went back upstairs, showered, and got ready, feeling only mildly guilty over the lie. I did have to get to work, just not for another couple of hours.

But I'd hated the way things had just ended with Liam, and I wanted to swing by the restaurant and maybe debrief or something. This had been an arrangement, but it still seemed like kind of an abrupt ending.

I walked over to Cagney's and spotted Adam as soon as I entered. I walked over to say hello, but he met me halfway across the restaurant floor.

"Maggie. So nice to see you. What can I do for you?" he asked.

"Actually, I'm looking for Liam. Is he in?"

Adam shook his head.

"No, he's not due for a little while. Should I tell him you came by?"

I nodded and we said our goodbyes. He walked back towards the kitchen and I was on my way out when I decided to stop and use the bathroom.

I was in the stall when I heard the door open and two women walk in. From their voices, and the fact that the restaurant was empty, I knew it was Bree and Toni.

"Whew. Liam is in fine form this morning," Toni said.

My heart soared. He was here. I smiled to myself, thinking fate had given me a small bladder just so I'd be here when he arrived.

"I know. Think it has to do with Maggie?" Task asked.

My ears perked up. Had he been talking about me? This was about to get interesting.

"No," Toni said. "I've asked him about her a

few times. He insists it's just an arrangement, that as soon as her folks leave, he's done."

My heart dropped and my mouth went dry.

"Figures," Bree said. "Some days I think that man will never grow up."

They laughed and exited the bathroom. I just sat there, unable to move. *He's done.* After a while, I got up, went to wash my hands, then cracked open the door and peered out. The last thing I wanted now was to run into Liam. If he wanted nothing to do with me, I certainly wanted nothing to do with him. He'd paid his debt, and he'd moved on. Fine.

CHAPTER SIXTEEN

Liam

There was nothing like a Saturday night in the kitchen of a happening restaurant to get your mind off your troubles. The orders were pouring in steadily from five o'clock until closing, leaving me no time to think about anything except plating the next meal.

Toni and I fell into our usual groove, and the line cook was kept on his toes all night. Bree would send back the occasional cocktail to keep us going.

It was close to eleven when we sent the last plate out. I pulled off my apron, glancing around at the kitchen and shooting the dishwasher an apologetic look.

"You can take home the leftover lobster," I told him. "There's enough there for a decent meal and there's nothing we can do with it here."

He smiled in gratitude and got back to work. It was a shit job, but it had its perks. Besides, we'd all been there.

"You coming out front?" Toni asked.

"Yeah. Be there in a minute."

Toni left the kitchen and headed to the bar. As the door closed behind her, I could hear the laughter and loud voices that only came from a crowd having a good time. I pulled out my phone and thought about texting Maggie. We'd left things kind of weirdly, and it wasn't sitting right with me.

Hey? You there?

I waited a few minutes but got no response, so I shoved the phone back in my pocket and headed to the bar.

*

I was three drinks in when Trish sat down next to me. Trish was a regular and often stuck around after hours to drink with the staff. Her daughter, Desi, was Adam's nanny/babysitter, and I'd once made the mistake of going home with her. Okay, twice.

She was a good time and everything, but she talked way too fucking much. Normally, I was good with conversation, but she never had anything of interest to say, so I found myself listening to step-by-step reenactments of her day. She ordered a drink from Bree and immediately launched into the killer meeting she'd had at work. The woman could be exhausting.

I nursed my scotch and it wasn't long before she turned her attention on me.

"What are you up to tonight, Chef?" she asked, a coy smile on her face.

"Sorry, Trish. Got plans tonight."

She pouted, then slid off the stool and went over to talk to a cluster of women. Toni came up beside me, studying me.

"What plans?"

I turned to her.

"Oh, none. Just not in the mood for that tonight."

"Since when?" she snorted.

I downed the rest of my drink and signalled Bree for another.

"Can't I just spend a fun night at work with my colleagues?"

"I guess. I just figured after a week of being caged, you'd be scratching to get out."

"It's not all about sex, you know."

Toni choked on her drink, set down her glass, then reached over to feel my forehead.

"Very funny," I murmured.

Bree delivered my drink and I pounded it down. I got off the stool, walked over to Trish, and whispered in her ear. She turned to me and smiled and together we left the bar.

*

I woke up the next morning on the living room floor of my apartment, still fully clothed, reeking of sweat and alcohol. I groaned as I rolled over onto my side, desperate to turn away from the window and all its light. I felt like I'd been hit by a truck. What the fuck had happened?

I ran my hand over my face, feeling the drool that had dried on the corner of my mouth. Great. A1, Liam.

"Fuck."

"Oh, are you awake?"

I sat straight up, banging my head on the coffee table. I simultaneously grunted, grabbed my head, and looked around to see who had spoken.

"Trish," I said, my head echoing with what sounded like thunder.

"Don't move. I'll make some coffee," she said, getting up off her perch on the couch and heading to the kitchen. "And get some ice."

"Thanks," I mumbled, still rubbing my head.

I frantically searched my memory, trying to piece the night together. I remembered working late, staying late, drinking a lot, and then—. *Oh, shit*. I glanced down, saw I was still in my clothes, and realized that nothing major could've happened.

Trish came back and handed me a bag of frozen peas, which I put on my head. Then she passed me two aspirin and a cup of steaming coffee. I'd never been so happy to have another human being around.

"What happened?" I asked.

"You just had too much to drink. By the time you figured out how to open the front door, you were done. One step into the apartment and you crashed. I forgot my purse at the restaurant, so I didn't have money for a cab. I slept on the couch."

"Shit. I'm sorry, Trish. Real class act, huh?"

She just smiled.

"That's okay. Can you spot me a tenner? I'm going to be late for work."

I reached into my back pocket for my wallet, extracted a twenty-dollar bill, and passed it over. She blew me a kiss and walked out the front door.

CHAPTER SEVENTEEN

Maggie

On Monday morning, I sent a brief text to Liam.

My folks are due back at noon. Can you spare an hour?

I was worried he wouldn't respond after I'd blown him off the other night when he'd texted me. But after a few minutes, his response came.

Sure. I'll be there by 11:50.

I briefly wondered how I was going to get through this lunch with my parents. I was grateful Justin would be joining us. He'd make a good buffer, and he wouldn't be at all confused about the tension.

I put together a quick charcuterie plate. I kept it simple, not wanting to compete with Liam's culinary skills. My father had already started talking about how nice it was to have someone around who actually knew how to cook a steak. I didn't need to sit through an hour of "why didn't you let Liam make lunch?"

At precisely ten to twelve, the door opened and I heard Liam call out.

"In here," I said.

Seconds later, he was beside me in the kitchen, peering into bowls and dishes.

"Looks good," he said.

"Thanks," I answered, not sure what to say.

I knew he didn't want to be there, and I felt bad about it, but he could've refused.

"Listen, thanks a lot for showing up today," I said.

"Hey, no sweat. Part of the deal, right?"

I looked down.

"Right." I wasn't sure what else to say. "Apartment good?"

"Yeah, it's great. Good to be home."

Okay, he didn't have to beat a dead horse. We were done. I got it. I put all the plates on a tray and walked them over to the dining room table. I moved the puzzle box of loose pieces to the side, laying out the food.

"Still working on this, huh?" he asked, fingering one of the pieces.

"I always have a puzzle going when I'm

writing."

He looked at me, curious.

"Why's that?"

I thought about it for a moment. I'd never tried to articulate it to another human being before.

"It helps me think. There's a process to doing a puzzle—it involves shapes and colour and I lose myself in it. If I'm stuck on a plot point, I can step away from the computer and escape into the puzzle. Just like the pieces in my hand, the parts come together in my mind." I paused. "Does that sound weird?"

"No. When did you start?" he asked.

"When I was a teenager. It was my escape from home life."

"You needed an escape? Even then?"

I nodded.

"Yeah. Justin was the golden child, and I was always being compared to him. It got to me. It affected my confidence in school, with friends…and with boys. I needed a way to transcend that whole experience. Putting those puzzles together gave me that. I know it's weird."

"Stop saying that. Everyone needs an out. I'm sorry you grew up like that. I just assumed you had the perfect childhood," he said. "I guess we've all got our shit to transcend."

"Is it true you don't speak to your family?" I asked.

"I really don't. I haven't spoken to my parents in years. They tried once, but they let me down. I'm not fool enough to let them do that again."

"You won't give them another chance?" I asked. "They are your parents. Don't you want a family?"

He shook his head.

"I'm fine on my own. I've got all I need."

I studied him for a moment, realization dawning on me.

"That's why you never have a girlfriend. Why you won't commit. You don't want to be let down."

The doorbell rang and I jumped, startled. A look of relief passed across Liam's face. I looked at him, then at the door, just as the bell rang again. I reluctantly walked over and opened it. My parents and Justin came in, chattering away about their weekend. I threw a glance at Liam, but he was busy rearranging the food. The moment was lost.

We sat down to eat, and my father kept nudging my mom not to dally, as he wanted to get back on the road before dark. Justin and Liam caught up, and I got to spend the entire meal in my little bubble, watching it all play out before me. I kept thinking about what Liam had told me, and his whole personality started making sense to me. He'd walled himself off on purpose.

As soon as we were done, my father stood, grabbed his car keys from the counter, and said, "Well, we're off."

"Where you headed now, Dad?" I asked, returning to the present.

"We're going to keep going west, see where the wind takes us. We'll call you from the road."

My mother grudgingly got up and walked over to say goodbye. She kissed me on the cheek, then pulled Justin in for a hug. My father hugged me and clapped Justin on the shoulder. But both of them went over to Liam and shook his hand, telling him how nice it had been to meet him.

A strained smile played at his lips and I silently willed my parents to hurry up and leave. As if psychic, my dad slapped my mom on the back and said, "Let's go."

And they were gone.

Once we heard the car retreat down the road, Liam grabbed his bag and headed for the door.

"Thanks," I called out as he turned the handle.

Without even looking back, he said, "No

sweat."

And then he was gone, too.

My brother and I stood in the kitchen, silent for a moment as we recovered from the visit. Finally, he turned to me.

"Well, that certainly went well. Mom and Dad LOVED Liam. I guess you get to stay."

"Yeah? You think they bought it?" I asked.

"For sure they bought it. They were talking about him all weekend. Well done, Mags. I gotta admit, I was worried about how it would all work out, but you pulled it off."

"I guess I did."

"Listen, I'm really sorry I got you involved with a guy like that. I just didn't know what else to do."

"It's fine, Justin. It worked, it's over, we can all go on with our lives."

Justin smiled and squeezed my shoulder. Then he leaned in and gave me a closer look.

"Did that motherfucker touch you?"

"Justin, shut up."

Before I could say another word, my brother was pacing the floor of my kitchen, mumbling under his breath about all the murderous acts he was about to commit.

"Justin! Stop! Nothing that happened was his fault. Stop it!"

He came to a stop right in front of me, inches

from my face.

"So something did happen?"

I opened my mouth to speak, then closed it again. I counted silently to ten while he stood there, glaring at me.

"I am a grown woman. I can make my own decisions. Whether something happened or not is none of your business. I think you just need to calm down."

I could see the steam escaping his ears as he listened to me, but I held my ground, not breaking eye contact. Finally, he relented. He let out a long breath and walked over to the front door.

"This isn't the end of this conversation. We will pick this up again."

CHAPTER EIGHTEEN

Liam

Judging by the fact that Justin didn't seem to give a fuck about the rather large knife in my hand as he stormed across the kitchen and grabbed me by the collar, I had to assume he was in a blind rage.

"Did you sleep with my sister?" he roared.

Adam and Toni discreetly disappeared. It had been two weeks since that horrible morning at Maggie's house.

"No," I said, standing stock still.

"But you fucking touched her. I told you not to touch her."

I pried his hand off my collar and took a step back. I was easily twice his strength.

"It's not what you think. Besides, she's a grown woman. She makes her own decisions."

Justin ran his hands through his hair and paced the kitchen floor.

"I want to fucking kill you, man," he said.

"I get it. I'm not too pleased with myself either."

"I spent two weeks trying to cool my jets, and then I get an email from my folks asking how Maggie's wonderful boyfriend is. She's my goddamn sister."

I put the knife down on the counter and sat down on the stool. Justin stopped pacing, picked up another stool, and brought it over to join me.

"What the fuck happened?" he asked.

"I don't know. I just wanted to do what you said, and things got a little out of hand."

"A little?" he asked, incredulous.

"Fine. A lot. Look, I don't know what she told you, but I've got nothing but respect for your sister, man. She's one of a kind. She's a good girl."

"Damn straight. Too good for you."

"I know that, man. I promise you, I'm not looking to mess around with her."

He gave me one last look and then disappeared as quickly as he'd shown up. Once he was gone, Toni slid back into the kitchen and walked up beside me.

"Everything okay?" she asked.

"It's fine. I wish everyone would just leave me the fuck alone."

The truth was, ever since Maggie had told me about her experience growing up, I'd felt like shit. Here was a great woman cursed with low self-esteem, and I basically screwed around with her then walked out. I couldn't have been a bigger shit if I'd tried. And I still couldn't work out why I cared so much.

*

I spent the next couple of weeks trying to get my groove back. It wasn't lost on me that it was taking me a month to get over a five-day... whatever. That last lunch together kept replaying in my mind. It was the first time we'd been real with each other. We exposed ourselves in a non-physical way, yet it felt ten times more intimate. I'd never told any woman about myself before, but with Maggie, it felt right. It felt natural.

The summer season was in full swing and the tourists and cottagers were everywhere. I spent the next two weeks working hard and then going out for a drink or two after work to wind down. Always with a crowd, but I always went home alone. It was never my intention—it just happened to work out that way.

One night I was taking off early after dinner and Adam stopped me, asking if I'd mind driving a case of cilantro out to Elena's, the Mexican joint on Highway 4.

"We're not going to use it, it'll go bad, and I owe her a favour. Do you mind?" he asked.

"Not at all. I've got nowhere else to be."

I took the case from him, threw it in the car, and headed out of town. It was a good plan. A new bar, fresh faces. Maybe tonight I'd turn things around.

It was close to ten when I pulled in outside the restaurant. The parking lot was full, which wasn't unusual for a Tuesday night in the summer months. Music was streaming out of the open door as people spilled out and others made their way inside. I drove around back and parked, making my way in through the kitchen door.

Elena saw me immediately and came over to relieve me of the case. She passed it off to the kitchen staff and pulled me into a hug.

"Liam, so good to see you. I hope you'll have a drink?" she asked.

"Absolutely. I'll find my way to the bar."

I gave her a kiss on the cheek and walked through the kitchen, greeting various acquaintances, and exited into the packed dining room. I made my way over to the bar and ordered a scotch. Within seconds, the empty stool on my right was taken by a tall blond holding an empty glass. She smiled at me and I signalled for the bartender.

"What are you drinking?" I asked her.

"Gin and tonic," she purred.

I ordered another round of drinks for both of us and we settled into easy conversation. Krissy grew up in Three Mountains, then left to go to school. She returned home a few summers ago and ended up working in a dress shop in Rocky Heights. Managing, she kept saying. She had aspirations of becoming a designer, so I wasn't sure what she was doing living outside of a major city, but I kept my mouth shut and enjoyed her company.

We were a few drinks in when Joe Jackson's *A Slow Song* came on. Krissy turned to me with a smile.

"Dance with me?" she said.

I got off the stool and took her hand as she slid off hers. I turned to the makeshift dance floor and saw Maggie, eyes closed, dancing with some skinny dude. I swallowed, a little unprepared for the conflicting thoughts going through my brain.

"What's the matter?" Krissy asked. "Let's go."

I turned to her.

"Second thought, why don't we take this dance outside?" I said.

She wrapped her arm around my waist and I steered her towards the side door, out into the parking lot. As soon as we were outside, she pulled me towards her and kissed me. I couldn't believe how long it had been since I'd kissed a woman, Maggie included. I'd been celibate for the past month. I hadn't gone that long without sex in over a decade. I was wired. And yet...

When Krissy kissed me, I felt nothing. I kissed her back, taking a handful of her hair in my fist and running my hand down the side of her neck. She moaned into my mouth, pressing herself up against me. *Nothing.* I wasn't sure what to do. That was a first. I always knew what to do.

Krissy, on the other hand, had zero qualms about what was going on. She was all in, running her hands under my shirt, up my back, scraping her nails across my skin. I couldn't even get it up. There was nothing there. Well, not nothing. Actually—

"Oh, shit!" I pulled away from Krissy and turned to the left before puking out the contents of the evening.

Krissy screeched and jumped back, putting

out her hands as if to shield herself from the back spray. Thankfully, there was none.

"Fuck. Dude. Seriously?"

She straightened her skirt and adjusted the spaghetti straps of her dress.

"I'm sorry. Really. I guess I just had too much too drink," I offered weakly.

"Yeah. Whatever."

She turned and walked back into the bar. I just stood there, staring at the door after it shut behind her.

CHAPTER NINETEEN

Maggie

Tammy and I were having lunch in the square outside the hotel. We'd gotten closer over the past few weeks, and it was nice to have a friend to hang out with. Spending that week with Liam around made me realize how lonely I'd been since moving to Mountain Valley. I was craving human companionship. As if reading my mind, Tammy looked up from her sandwich and considered me.

"What are you doing tonight? Writing?" she asked.

"Nope. Sent the manuscript off to publishers. Now it's a waiting game," I said.

"Perfect. Come out with me tonight. I've got a date, but I'm sure he can rustle up a friend."

I thought about it for less than a minute.

Why not? I'd spent enough time over the past few weeks doing nothing. Liam was out of my life, but that didn't mean I couldn't go in search of other research candidates, so to speak. I smiled.

"I'm in."

*

Sure enough, Tammy's date, Eric, found a willing friend. Shane was tall with curly blond hair and a slight frame. He was cute and had an amazing smile.

We met at the Mexican place on Highway 4. I'd never been before, but both their margaritas and their jukebox were legendary. I put on a summer dress for the occasion, blue with tiny white polka dots and spaghetti straps. I couldn't bring myself to wear heels, but I did put on a little makeup.

We sat at a table for four and ordered pitchers of margaritas and a plate of tacos. It was noisy, but we were still able to carry on a decent conversation. Shane worked at the local bookstore, which explained why he'd looked familiar when we were introduced.

"I recognized you right away," he said,

smiling at me. "Romance section. Two to four books a week."

I laughed, delighted. Tammy shot me a knowing look and then dragged Eric onto the makeshift dance floor. Shane and I sat silently for a few minutes, drinking and watching people dance.

"So what do you do?" he asked.

"Well, by day I work with Tammy at The Elway, but at night I have a secret identity as a romance writer."

"Ah," he said. "That explains all the novels. Research, huh?"

The smile dropped from my face at the word *research*. For the first time that evening, I thought of Liam. I closed my eyes and took a breath, but all I could see was his hand, moving up my thigh. My eyes flew open, only to find Shane studying me with an odd expression.

"You okay? I say something wrong?"

"Not at all," I assured him.

I took a sip of my drink, trying to remember if this was my second or third. I was certainly feeling no pain, and I was proud of myself for going out, making friends, and finally letting loose. Joe Jackson's *A Slow Song* came on the jukebox.

"I love this song," I said.

Shane stood up and reached out his hand.

"Then let's dance."

I took his hand and followed him to the dance floor. He wrapped his arms around my waist and I draped mine over his shoulders. My first thought was he was so much skinnier than Liam, and my second thought was he wasn't Liam. It made me irrationally sad. Why was I even still thinking about him? I blamed it on the alcohol and closed my eyes. I leaned my head against his shoulder and as we swayed to the music, I tried to let myself enjoy the moment for what it was.

When the song ended, I pulled away and looked up at him to thank him for the dance. Before I could say anything, he leaned down to kiss me. It was a soft, gentle kiss. It was fine. But there was zero magic. I pulled away, running my thumb over my bottom lip.

"Thank you for the dance," I said.

His expression fell.

"Just the dance."

"Hey. I'm having a great time with you tonight. Really."

He nodded, took my hand, and guided me back to the table. Tammy and Eric had ordered another pitcher and were pouring more drinks. I suddenly felt awkward and out of place. I'd had more to drink than I should've and for a few moments, I'd let myself believe I was someone I wasn't.

I pulled out my phone and checked the black screen.

"Shit," I murmured.

Tammy looked up.

"What's up?" she asked.

"It's Justin. Says it's an emergency. Listen, I've got to run. He's going to come pick me up. I'll see you tomorrow, okay?"

Tammy jumped up and gave me a quick hug. She pulled me close and whispered in my ear.

"I know exactly what you're doing."

I let go of her, told Eric it had been nice to meet him, then turned to Shane.

"Listen—" I started.

He held up his hand.

"If you want, get my number from Tammy."

I smiled, gave them all a last wave, and headed out to the parking lot, calling a cab on the way.

CHAPTER TWENTY
Liam

I woke up the next morning in my car, still parked in Elena's lot. I had a raging hangover, my mouth was full of cotton, and a sinking realization settled in my gut. I had a thing for Maggie.

There was no other explanation. My lack of screwing around, my reaction to making out with Krissy, the tenderness I'd felt towards Maggie when she shared her childhood with me, and of course, that feeling of utter despair when I saw her dancing with that fuckhead.

I sat up, hitting my head on the roof of the car. *Shit.* I was going to pay for that later when full sensation returned to my body. I looked around, but the parking lot was empty. Small mercies. I pulled the seat up into driving position and strapped myself in.

I stopped at the gas station for coffee before hitting the highway. I'd never driven so slowly in my life. By the time I was halfway back to Mountain Valley, I could barely see through the pounding behind my temples. Thankfully, I wasn't due at the restaurant until eleven, so I had time to get home, shower, and pop some aspirin. I knew it would be another crazy day ahead. At least it would give me a reprieve from my thoughts. Fucking Maggie.

*

I made it to work on time, but I looked even worse than I felt, and I felt pretty crappy. Bree eyed me as I walked past the bar.

"Don't even ask," I said and kept walking.

I washed up in the kitchen and tied on my apron, pulling down a copy of the day's dinner menu to get started on prep while Toni took care of the lunch crowd. We did not have a traditional arrangement in the kitchen, but it worked for us, and everything had been running smoothly since her arrival. She was a godsend. Or rather, a Justin send, as I was so keenly aware these days.

We stayed out of each other's way until the lunch rush was over, and then Toni came over to give me a hand.

"You look like a piece of shit," she said.

"Thanks."

"That my dog stepped in and then dragged across my floor," she continued.

"Okay. I get the point."

"Rough night?"

"Not in the way you think. Drank too much and passed out in my car in the parking lot of Elena's," I confessed.

"Shit. What's up, Liam? Talk to me."

I put down my knife, carefully wrapped the cuts of beef I'd been slicing, and put them away in the walk-in before answering her.

"I think I'm in trouble," I began.

"Oh crap. What did you do? Did you hit someone? We'll figure it out, don't worry."

"Toni, shit, I didn't drive drunk. But I think I might...fuck, I can't believe I'm about to say this...I think I might like a woman."

"Maggie?" she asked, without any trace of a real question.

"Yeah. Shit. That obvious?" I asked.

"Chef, you have not been the same person since that woman walked into your life. First, you came alive like we'd never seen you, then you shut down, then you just went nuts. The three of us feel like we've been watching a tornado blow through here for the past month.

What happened with you two?"

I told her. I told her the absolute truth. That I'd done this favour for Justin that turned into this super hot research project that just fucking ended. And that somewhere along the way, I'd fallen for the girl.

"And that's it?" she asked.

"Yeah. We were both pretty clear about the terms of the agreement."

She rolled her eyes.

"But she enjoyed the sex?"

"Fuck, yeah."

"So what makes you think she's not interested?"

"Well, I'm not exactly her type. Plus, I tried texting her and she never responded. And then last night—"

"What the hell happened last night?"

I took her through the gory details. After she finished laughing, she gave me crap for not having gone over to talk to Maggie at the bar.

"It really wasn't appropriate. She was dancing pretty close with the dude. It would've been more than awkward."

"Okay," she conceded. "Point taken. So? Call her. Ask her out."

I shook my head.

"She wants nothing to do with me. Transaction complete."

"Hmm. Normally I'd say to leave it alone then, but I saw the two of you together. There was definitely something there. You just need to find an in."

"And where do you suppose I do that? Got any suggestions?"

"Let me think on it," she said. "Right now, I'm outta here. Have fun with the dinner crowd."

*

We were closed for Canada Day on July 1, and I took the opportunity to sleep until noon. I'd stayed late at the restaurant the night before, nursing a scotch while Adam, Toni, and Bree amused themselves by trying to find solutions to my situation.

"I just can't believe someone finally got to you," Adam said. "I was starting to think you were going to carry on like that forever."

"Hey, boss, I'm in my thirties, not my fifties. And I'm not talking about getting married here. I just want to get to know the woman."

"Uh, huh," he said, smiling.

"Listen, just because you're all cozy with Tess doesn't mean we all want a long-term commitment. I've got a thing for this girl. I just want to see where it goes. If I can ever figure out a way to get near her."

"You gotta make her think it's her idea," he said. "Tess's friend Jax told me that when I was trying to figure out how to convince her to date me. Worked for us."

I thought about that as I rolled over in bed and stared at the ceiling. I had zero plans for the day, figuring I'd laze about, whip up some dinner, then head to the square to see the fireworks. Bree and I had made a plan to meet there. She was still relatively new to the area and hadn't hooked up with anyone yet. She told me she'd split with her last boyfriend shortly before moving. In fact, it had been the impetus for her move.

My buzzer rang and I glanced at the phone on my night table to check the time. Almost one. Who the hell was popping by at one o'clock on a day off? I rolled out of bed and walked to the front door, pulling on a pair of sweats on the way. I hit the buzzer to let them in, then opened the door and looked out into the hall.

I saw Toni coming up the staircase with two large shopping bags, one in each hand. They looked heavy as fuck so I dashed out into the hall to take them from her, peeking inside in the process.

"May I ask—"

"You may, as soon as we get inside," Toni said, cutting me off.

I followed her into the apartment and shut the door. She kicked off her shoes and walked into the kitchen, searching the fridge for a drink. She was right at home, having roomed with me for a few weeks while she looked for a place of her own. She had no desire to drive the thirty minutes to work every morning if she'd stayed where she was, so as soon as she took the job with us, she'd moved to Mountain Valley.

The first thing she said when she walked into my place that first time was, "I'm never going to sleep with you." She'd been true to her word. She's the first female friend I'd ever had. I never looked at her in a sexual way, though she was smoking hot. I was grateful for her every fucking day, though. Especially today.

"Okay, tell me," I said.

She pulled herself up onto a stool and popped open seltzer. She took a long drink and set the can down.

"So, you got yourself a romance writer who doesn't believe in the glory of sex. And you're a sex machine who doesn't believe in romance. But you were able to change her mind about sex. Maybe we just need to change your mind about romance."

"What the fuck are you getting at?" I asked.

She walked over to the shopping bags and dumped them out on the living room floor.

"Romance novels," she declared. "My entire collection. Okay, fine, half my collection."

I looked at her, incredulous.

"FINE. A quarter of my collection. But enough to suit your purposes. I pulled out the tropes I thought would be appropriate—friends to lovers, enemies to lovers, fake relationships—"

"Wait. That's a thing? The fake relationship? That's a plot device?"

"Oh yes," Toni said dreamily. "One of the best, too."

"Jesus Christ, I'm living in a romance novel."

"At least yours has great sex."

"Had."

"Which brings me back to my point. You've got the day off? Start reading. See what you can pick up. She's not interested because she thinks you're a certain type of guy. Show her you're not that guy. Show her you're exactly the guy she's looking for."

I turned one of the books over in my hand, glancing at the blurb on the back but mildly distracted by the side boob on the cover.

"Well, I guess it couldn't hurt," I said.

"Fantastic," she said, flopping down on the couch beside me. "Order some pizza before you get started. I brought the weed."

CHAPTER TWENTY-ONE

Maggie

"You have plans for the fireworks tonight?" Tammy asked.

"Well, I was planning to go," I answered.

"With who?"

"I was just going to walk over after dark. I don't know. I didn't really make a plan," I admitted.

Tammy just rolled her eyes.

"I'm going with Eric. Come with us. I can ask him to invite Shane if you want…"

"That's okay. But I will meet you there."

"No Shane?"

"No Shane."

She eyed me.

"You still hung up on the chef?"

"Absolutely not!"

"Tell me."

I thought about it for a moment, but only a moment. Tammy was a friend, and if I couldn't talk to her, who could I talk to?

"We fooled around," I said.

"I KNEW IT!" she screamed.

I looked around at all the faces that turned to stare at us.

"Quieter, please," I begged.

"I knew it," she hissed. "You slept with him."

"I didn't, actually. We never got that far."

And with that, I told her the whole story. She listened, amazed.

"Wow. And no strings attached?"

"None," I said.

"Any regrets?" she asked.

"None. It was amazing. Now I just need to find a decent guy who's able to do those same things—"

"Hmm. I see the issue. Why not Shane?"

I sighed.

"Because when he kissed me, I felt nothing."

"Ah."

*

After a decadent take-out meal from the local Italian place, I took a quick shower, tied up my hair, and put on a bit of makeup. I rifled through my closet and pulled out a black, short-sleeve wrap dress. A pair of comfortable flats and I was ready to go.

I texted Tammy as soon as I got to the square. There were so many people out—residents, tourists, and seasonal renters alike—that it would be near impossible to find her in the crowd. There were different bands set up in different areas of the square, far enough away from each other that they'd each attracted their own crowd.

I saw a bunch of people I knew, including the crew from Franni's bakery—Tess, Katie, Jax, and Chance. I'd become a regular at that place and they were all super friendly. Katie's boyfriend, the actor Mason Scott, was with them but by this point, he was becoming a regular fixture in the town and not stirring up much fuss. Except amongst the tourists.

I made my way towards our meeting spot and saw Tammy standing with Eric, the two of them laughing over some private joke. I felt a momentary stab and wondered if maybe I should've given Shane another shot. I hadn't been lonely before, but now that I'd had a taste of both the company and the sexual possibility, I wanted more.

"Hey, you two," I said as I approached.

"Mags!" Tammy threw her arms around me.

"Hey, Maggie," Eric said.

I smiled at him as I pulled away from Tammy.

"I didn't realize I'd be the third wheel here. I'm sorry," I said.

"Don't be ridiculous. We're happy to have you along. And there are plenty of people here, nudge, nudge." Tammy winked at me to reinforce her point.

We found ourselves a good spot on the grass and I spread out the blanket I'd brought. Tammy and I sat down and Eric went off to find us refreshments.

*

The Mayor was wrapping up her speech just as we were finishing our second round of drinks. Tammy was off doing a tour of the food trucks and Eric was anxious she wouldn't get back in time for the fireworks. There was a slight chill in the air so I pulled my cardigan out of my bag and threw it over my shoulders.

"That's it," Eric said. "I'm going to look for her."

"Are you serious? If you leave, she'll just show up. Did you try texting her?" I asked.

"Of course. She probably can't hear her

phone in the crowd."

Eric got to his feet and disappeared into a swarm of people. I stretched out on the blanket, laid down on my back, and stared up at the stars. It was a clear night and the effect was magical. It was like everyone else melted away and it was just me and the universe. Me and the skies. I watched a shooting star, so much more common up here than I'd ever realized, but no less miraculous because of it.

I was in my own world when the first firework went off overheard. I couldn't help but smile. I loved fireworks. The lights, the music, the show, even the smell. The next set went off and I laid there, transfixed.

Until my vision was blocked by a grinning face. A very familiar grinning face. I sat up.

"Liam."

"Hey, Maggie. Mind if I join you?"

I looked around, aware for the first time that neither Eric nor Tammy had made their way back to the blanket. I had no acceptable reason for saying no, so I indicated the space beside me and he sat down.

"How you been?" he asked.

"Okay. You?"

"Great. Working hard."

"Well, if the occupancy rate at the hotel is any indication of the business you're doing, I imagine so," I said.

"Yeah." He was silent for a moment, watching the sky. "Listen, I don't know what happened—"

"Nothing happened. Forget about it," I said.

"Yeah?"

"Yeah."

We sat there, together, watching the rest of the fireworks in silence, save for the obligatory oohs and aahs. I wondered who he'd come with, or if he'd come alone. If he'd abandoned his party to come sit with me, and if so, why? I couldn't piece together his reasoning and he was offering no clues, just sitting there quietly beside me.

He shifted position, and his arm brushed against mine. I felt tingles along my skin where we'd made contact. I swallowed, hoping he wouldn't notice, and casually moved my arm away. There was definitely chemistry. I chewed the inside of my lip as I contemplated my options. Would one more night with Liam, a chance to finish what we'd started, be a terrible idea or a brilliant one?

By this point, my vagina was doing the thinking. I was well aware of that, but the longer he sat by me, the more tension built between us. I could feel his hands on me, his breath on my neck, his tongue in my—

"Liam? There you are!"

We both turned to see a woman, mid-fifties, standing about five feet in front of us. Liam closed his eyes, the classic *Oh, shit* look crossing his face. Had he been on a date?

"Trish. Hey. Do you know Maggie Grant? Maggie, this is Trish."

Trish and I looked each other over and smiled politely.

"You just disappeared on us, Liam. I was wondering what happened," Trish said.

"I'm all good, thanks. Tell Adam I'll be in tomorrow, okay?"

Trish stood there, looking stung. She looked over at me again with a new appreciation and a not-so-polite smile. Then she turned and walked away.

"Your date?" I asked.

"No, no, that's just..." He trailed off, never really finishing the sentence. I didn't need him to. Her presence had been a reminder of who I was dealing with. If anything, I should thank her for showing up. She'd probably saved me from a huge mistake.

CHAPTER TWENTY-TWO

Liam

"Fuck, fuck, FUCK!" I brought down the knife with controlled fury, splitting the rabbit carcass in two with one clean slice.

"I'm guessing it didn't go well," Bree whispered to Toni a few feet behind me.

"I can hear you. I'm right fucking here."

"I said," Bree said, raising her voice. "I'm guessing it didn't go well last night."

"No, it didn't." I put the knife down on the chopping block and turned to face the two of them. "It was going fine, then Trish came along, and that threw everything into a tailspin. Fucking Trish."

Toni walked up to me and put her finger right in my face.

"Don't you dare blame Trish for this. You

155

lived your life how you wanted to for thirty-odd years? Own it. Trish wouldn't treat you the way she does if you didn't let her. You're a fucking boy toy. You want to change? Change."

She turned on her heel and walked out of the kitchen. I turned to look at Bree, who just shrugged and followed Toni out to the bar. I turned back to my rabbit.

The thing was, she was right. This had nothing to do with Trish. This was all on me.

Maybe owning that was the first step in a new direction.

When I got home that night, I sat on my couch, pulled out my cell phone, and deleted the contact information for every single one of my hook-ups. Some hurt a little to let go but mostly what I felt was relief. Then I tossed my phone onto the couch, leaned over, and grabbed a new book off the pile on the floor.

*

I spent the week devouring those novels. I'd work long hours, come straight home, and read until I crashed. My phone rang a few times, and I made the mistake of answering twice. I hadn't realized how many women I'd been involved with and it would take a while to separate myself from the ill-conceived reputation I'd built.

Toni had done a remarkably good job of whittling the selection. There was something useful in every one of the books I read. It wasn't lost on me, though, that the more I read, the more I found it like porn. It was all right there on the page—the impossible scenarios, the unattainable expectations. What man could possibly live up to these guys? Certainly no man I'd ever met. But, despite that, I kept reading, because idiot that I was, even I was smart enough to realize that there was a kernel of truth in every one of those ridiculous tales.

"Do you remember the one where the couple had to pretend to be married in order to qualify for school housing?" I asked Toni as we worked side-by-side plating dishes.

"Liam, I'm legit starting to worry about you. You realize these are fantasy, right? Not real life."

"Yeah, whatever, I'm still getting good stuff."

Toni passed her plate off to the server and wiped her hands on her apron. We were at the tail end of the dinner rush and I suspect I was pissing her off.

"Like what?" she asked.

"Well, that women want to be treated with

respect, that I should ask more questions and listen more than I talk, that it's important to give them their space—"

"Shit," she interrupted. "You really are learning something. Okay, tell me about the fake marriage for the student housing. Refresh my memory."

Stella, the server, was standing there listening attentively. I glared at her and she took her plates and returned to the dining room. Somehow, over the past week, my personal life had become everyone's pet project.

"So anyway, in that one, the guy decorates the entire apartment with everything she loves, so she'll know he really wants her to stay," I said.

"Right. That was a good one."

"I was thinking, what if I did something like that for Maggie? I mean, not decorate her fucking house, but maybe just somehow show her I'm taking an interest in the things she likes, or whatever."

"Like what?" Toni asked.

"Well, fuck, I don't know. I hadn't gotten that far," I admitted.

I pulled off my apron after the last plate went out and scrounged for food. Poking around in the pots, I found a little crab risotto leftover and dished some out before turning the rest over to the staff.

"Books. She loves reading," I said. "Maybe I could take her to the bookstore."

"And get her to recommend some books for you?" Toni suggested.

"Shit, that's a great idea."

Toni laughed and rolled her eyes.

"Let me know how it goes."

*

On Saturday, during the afternoon lull, I took a walk over to Maggie's hotel. I made a quick stop along the way at the bookstore, popping in to buy a hundred-dollar gift card. The skinny dude behind the cash took my money and I left the shop, pleased with my plan.

When I hit the hotel, I found a bench across the street in the square, right in the line of sight of the door. It was three o'clock, her day was just ending, and there was no way she'd miss me when she walked out. I pulled out my phone and pretended to look busy while I waited. It took about ten minutes, but sure enough, she came out. Dressed in jean shorts and a red T-shirt, she looked incredible. Hair tied back, freckles having multiplied in the sun —I hadn't seen her in daylight in a while and it took my breath away.

She glanced over and our eyes locked. She gave me a hesitant smile then made her way across the street towards me. I patted the empty seat on the bench and she sat down.

"Hi," she said.

"Hi, yourself."

"This a coincidence?" she asked.

"Not quite," I admitted. "I had a situation and I thought maybe you could help me out."

She raised an eyebrow.

"And here I thought we were done helping each other out."

Ouch.

"Fair. How about this, then? An exchange."

"I'm listening."

"A client at the restaurant gave me a gift card as a thank you the other day. I'd like your help spending it."

"Okay. I'm intrigued."

"It's for the bookstore. I'm not much of a reader, but I thought maybe you could help me pick out a few things. As a thank you, you can grab a book, too."

She practically leaped off the bench.

"Deal! Let's go."

"Right now?" I asked.

"Right now," she confirmed.

I checked my phone. I had another hour

before I had to be back at the restaurant. What the hell? I stood up and together we crossed the street and made our way over. It was only as we were about to enter that I caught the flaw in this plan. The skinny dude behind the counter. *Shit.*

CHAPTER TWENTY-THREE
Maggie

We walked into the bookstore and Mrs. Fairfax, the elderly woman who ran the place, was behind the register, organizing some new hardcovers on a shelf. She turned when she heard us come in, then smiled as I approached.

"Maggie! So nice to see you again," she said.

I smiled and turned to Liam, waiting to introduce him.

"Liam, this is Mrs. Fairfax. She could've helped you, too. But I'm greedy and want the free book. Mrs. Fairfax, this is Liam, the chef over at Cagney's."

Liam reached over and shook hands with the owner of the small book shop, an almost relieved-looking smile on his face. *What was that about?*

"Is there anything I can do for you? Your order hasn't come in yet, dear," Mrs. Fairfax said.

"I know. I'm just here to help Liam pick out a few books. We won't be long."

I turned to ensure he was following me, then made my way towards the non-fiction section.

"What's all this?" he asked, looking around.

"This is the biography section. True stories about real people, either written by the people themselves, or by a second party. Pick a chef."

"Anthony Bourdain."

"Easy," I said, and pulled a paperback down off the shelf.

No Reservations. He flipped it over and read the back.

"Another," I said.

"Ruth Reichl. Not really a chef, but a great restaurant critic."

I spun around, focused on a row of books, and let my finger trail along their spines until I found what I was looking for. *Tender at the Bone*. Again, I handed it to Liam, who flipped it and read the description. Two minutes and he already had two books.

"You're good at this," he said.

I rolled my eyes.

"It doesn't take any special talent to find books that you tell me you're interested in."

"Fine," he said. "Then recommend something."

I smiled at the challenge and started wandering through the stacks. He followed a few paces behind, giving me the space and silence required to make such a selection. I finally settled on a copy of Douglas Adams' *Last Chance to See*. As I turned to hand it to him, Shane came around the corner.

"Maggie!" he said.

"Shane, so good to see you."

He reached over and gave me an awkward hug. Awkward both because Liam was standing right there, and awkward because of the way we'd left things at Elena's that night. I pulled away and turned to Liam, pulling him forward.

"Liam, this is Shane, Shane, Liam—"

"Yeah, actually—" Shane started.

"Yeah, actually, I think we may have met somewhere before. You look familiar, man," Liam said, glaring at Shane.

Shane let out a short laugh and nodded his head.

"Yeah. Someplace." Shane turned to me. "Listen, if there's anything you need—"

"We're good, thanks. I don't want to keep you from your work."

He smiled and walked past us, and I handed

the book to Liam, feeling the buzz of my phone in my pocket. I pulled it out, intending to turn it off. My parents.

"Shit. They've been calling non-stop. Actually, it's good you're here. Would you mind saying hello? They've been asking about you."

Liam reached out and took the phone from my hand, answering the call.

"Hello? Maggie's phone. Mrs. Grant! So good to hear your voice! No, no, I've just been busy at the restaurant. Maggie? Yeah, she's here. She was just busy with something so I grabbed the phone. Hold on, I'll pass you over. Okay. You take care, too."

He smiled as he tossed the phone back to me, clearly pleased with himself. I was grateful. They'd been on my back for weeks about him — Where's Liam? How come we never speak to Liam? This was the best thing that could've happened.

I put the phone to my ear and listened as my mother ran through her weekly news. I wasn't paying attention and almost missed the last part.

"What?" I said. "Can you repeat that, please?"

"Sure thing, honey. Sunday night. We'll be there Sunday night and we'll leave Monday afternoon. We decided to loop back around instead of going directly home. Some stuff on the East Coast we want to explore. We'll only be with you one night."

It felt like all the breath had been knocked out of me. Liam was staring at me as he paid for the books with his gift card. Then he took my hand and guided me outside into the fresh air. I was just hanging up the phone as we hit the sidewalk.

"What was that all about?" he asked.

"They're coming back. Monday."

A surprised look crossed his face.

"For how long?" he asked.

"Just one night. We can say you're out of town."

"They'll never believe that. It's the height of the tourist season. Where the hell would I be?"

"Shit." I wracked my brain, trying to figure out how I was going to spin this, when Liam reached out and took my hands.

"Hey. It's okay. I'll stay the night."

I looked up at him, disbelieving.

"Really?"

He nodded.

"Why would you do that?"

He shrugged.

"I dunno. Got nothing better to do. And we didn't come this far just to blow it for one night."

Without a thought, I threw my arms around his waist and hugged him hard. He was stiff at first, surprised, but he quickly recovered, wrapping his arms around me and hugging me back.

Without letting go, I whispered, "I didn't get my book."

He laughed softly.

"I'll give you the rest of the gift card."

Neither of us had let go.

CHAPTER TWENTY-FOUR

Liam

I couldn't believe my luck. If I'd tried, I wouldn't have been able to plan it better. When I saw that skinny fuck in the bookstore, and then realized it was the same dude she'd been dancing with at Elena's, I figured my chances were shot. But she'd blown him off, and the day had gone well. Until the phone call.

But in the end, that phone call was everything. It was my ticket back in. I was standing at the stove, checking on the demiglace to make sure it was reducing properly, shaking my head in disbelief.

"And how do you plan to play this?" Adam asked.

By this point, no one was even being discreet anymore. My social life had become the staff project. Everyone had a fucking comment or suggestion. It was driving me nuts, but I tried to take it in stride. Toni and her big mouth. But I couldn't be mad at her. I was too crazy about her.

"I'm not worried. We've spent the night together before. The woman can't resist me," I said. "Correction, we can't resist each other."

"Hey, hey, hey," Toni said, dipping her finger in the sauce. "Back up, Chef. You are not going to touch her. Sauce is perfect, you're a genius."

"What do you mean, I'm not going to touch her? That's my fucking secret weapon."

She shook her head while the rest of the staff looked on in disbelief.

"Chef. You're trying to show her you're not that guy. You need to win her heart, not her pussy. Remember what Adam said—make her come to you. It's got to be her idea," Toni said.

I glanced over at Adam and he nodded.

"So what do you suggest?" I asked the room.

The dishwasher poked his head up from his station in the corner and offered, "Just be honest. Tell her how you feel."

I stood there, stunned. That wasn't covered in any of the romance novels. I looked around to get a consensus, and everyone was nodding in agreement.

"Toni?" I asked.

"Yeah. It makes sense."

Just then, the first server walked in with an order and we all got back to our stations, revving up for the night.

*

First thing Monday morning, I called Maggie.

"Hey, I had an idea. Why don't we meet at the grocery store and we'll pick up some stuff for dinner? I'll cook for your folks and we'll make a fun evening of it."

There was silence for a moment and I wondered if I'd made a bad call. Had we reached this level of friendship yet? Was I overplaying my hand? And when the hell did I start overthinking shit like this?

"Never mind, it was just an idea—"

"No," she interjected. "It's a great idea. Let's meet in an hour."

I smiled, said goodbye, and hung up the phone. Then I jumped in the shower.

*

She was waiting for me by the front entrance of Lester's General Store, the only real grocery store in town. It had a surprisingly good

170

produce section and whenever I couldn't make it up to the farm I stopped in. Lester also ran a great butcher shop. Over the years, the residents in Mountain Valley had changed and now they wanted better food, so he adapted. At least that's what he told me.

Maggie looked stunning, as always. She had such an easy beauty to her. She never did anything, never wore anything special—she just exuded warmth, and that made her beautiful. I couldn't imagine what she'd looked like all dressed up, going somewhere formal. I caught myself hoping I'd get a chance one day to find out.

Never had a woman affected me like this before. I liked women, I had a healthy respect for them, and normally, an insatiable appetite as well. But I hadn't even thought about sex with anyone else since I'd met her. And when I was spending time with her, I wasn't even trying to work out ways to get her into bed. She made me laugh. She made me think. She—

Oh, fuck.

CHAPTER TWENTY-FIVE
Maggie

I didn't know how to feel about this plan when Liam called me. I was grateful that he was doing me the favour, but I wasn't exactly keen on spending any additional time with him. Once I'd decided he wasn't right for me, I had no interest in being in such close proximity to something I'd never have. Sure, the past few times we'd seen each other had been enjoyable. Fun, even. I'd seen a side of him I'd never seen before, and that was nice. But that's all it was. Nice.

But in the end, grocery shopping with Liam turned out to be an adventure. I shouldn't have been surprised. He told me so much about the different fruits and vegetables as we strolled the produce section. The properties of each, how he prepared them, what dishes he used them in. We had a similar experience at the butcher counter, where he explained the different cuts of beef, and how to know which pieces demanded to be roasted, braised, or grilled.

It was a fascinating escape into his world, and I loved watching him light up as he talked about food. It was clear how passionate he was on the topic. He dragged me into the spice section, showing me his favourites and letting me in on some of his chef secrets.

"How do you know when bread is ready?" I asked.

"Knock on the bottom. Should sound hollow."

I nodded, eager for more.

"And how do you know how long to cook one of those massive cuts of meat?"

"Depends on the cut and desired level of doneness. It's an x number of minutes per pound equation."

"Amazing," I muttered.

He grabbed my hand and dragged me to the dairy counter, where he had me try a variety of different cheeses. It seemed when you were a top chef and you shopped in the local stores, they were more than willing to let you sample. It was like my own private Saturday morning at Costco.

By the time we hit the checkout line, we were both in a great mood, laughing and enjoying each other's company. The dread I'd been feeling about the impending evening was quickly being replaced by anticipation.

*

By the time we got back to my place, it was already five o'clock. Liam got set up in the kitchen, then called me in to play sous-chef.

"This is ridiculous," I said. "I mean, I can cook, but I can't chop like you want me to chop these."

I was staring helplessly at a pile of carrots that he expected me to cut in these perfect diagonal ovals. He'd demonstrated for me earlier, but I'd been distracted by the way his muscles moved as he brought the knife down. It was unsettling having him back in my kitchen. I didn't think having him around would affect me like this, but as soon as he stepped into my house, my body turned on. I put down the knife and went to open a bottle of wine.

"I gave you a knife demo last time I was here. Haven't you been practicing?" he asked, a chastising tone in his voice.

I poured myself a glass and took a sip before pouring one for him. I passed it over, but he just took it and set it on the counter.

"Come here," he said.

I walked over to him, anticipation heavy with each step. I could smell him and it was driving me crazy. He took my wrist, then guided me to the counter, getting behind me and wrapping his arms around my waist.

"Just like this," he said, picking up the knife and showing me how it's done.

I allowed myself a fraction of a second to melt into his chest. He stiffened, and I instantly regretted it. I stood up straighter, but his arm came around my waist, pulling me closer once more. I turned my head to look at him, and we just stood there, gazing into each other's eyes. Desire enveloped us. I saw it in his eyes, and I knew mine reflected the same. He dropped the knife on the counter and took my chin in his hand.

Then the doorbell rang.

We both jumped apart as if caught in some illicit act. My heart was beating so fast I thought it would rip out of my chest.

"My parents," I muttered.

"Yeah," he said, running his hand through his hair. "Of course."

I backed away from him until I hit the

counter, then turned and went to answer the door. My parents barreled in, laden with shopping bags and the overpowering scent of pine air freshener. Way too much time in the RV.

"Maggie, so good to see you, sweetheart!" My mother pulled me in for a hug while my father slapped me on the back and went straight towards Liam.

"Liam, I told Maggie to have you call. You'll never believe this incredible spice mix I found at this roadside stand. Unreal."

My dad and Liam retreated to the kitchen to talk shop and finish prepping dinner. I stood by the door with my mother while she sorted out her multitude of shopping bags. There was another knock on the door and it cracked open, Justin sticking his head inside.

"Saw the RV and figured it was safe to assume you were here," he said, giving my mother a hug and a quick kiss on the cheek.

"Hey," I said. "I didn't know you were coming."

I went over and hugged him.

"Justin? Is that you?" my father called from the kitchen, even though they were in direct line of sight.

My brother gave my shoulder and squeeze and shot me a quizzical look before nodding his chin towards Liam. *Later,* I mouthed. He nodded once then went over to say hi to dad. Since Justin and Liam were now available, my mom and I decided to take a walk while the men finished making dinner.

The weather was lovely, a perfect July day. Having stopped for a few minutes to take a breather, it was hard to believe how much I'd packed into the past few hours.

"I've got to tell you, Maggie, I'm surprised at how much I like Liam," my mother said, breaking the silence.

"What's that supposed to mean? That no decent man would be attracted to me?"

"No, it's just, well, the tattoos, the overall look—for someone who has steered clear of dating for a while, he seemed an odd choice. I was worried maybe you were just rebelling. But the more I get to know him, the more I like him. You did good, sweetheart. I'm happy you're happy."

"I am happy, but that doesn't mean he's the one, Mom. We're having a great time together, but things do change." I figured it best to prepare her.

"Oh, no. I can see it in the way you two look at each other. He's crazy about you. Just as crazy as you are about him."

We walked, our footsteps crunching on the

pine-strewn path through the woods by the coach house. The trail was one of my favourite parts of living here. Anytime I needed to get back in touch with myself, refocus my energy, I had this glorious trail through the woods literally outside my front door. It offered a different sanctuary than the jigsaw puzzles.

"We've been having a bit of trouble lately," I ventured.

I'm not sure why I said it. I guess I was longing for that mother-daughter bonding moment where she would give me all sorts of great advice. She gave me a sympathetic look and took my hand.

"I told you, dear. He's a good man. Just do what makes him happy."

So much for that.

CHAPTER TWENTY-SIX
Liam

I was determined to do everything right. I repeated the steps in my head like I was memorizing a recipe. A spoonful of affection, a cup of chivalry, a dash of romance. I worked my way through dinner prep in a bubble, only coming out occasionally to give instructions to Justin or his father.

When Maggie got back from her walk with her mom, I was ready. I met her at the door with a glass of her favourite red wine and kissed the top of her forehead. She blinked, surprised, and thanked me before taking a sip. I felt her eyes on my back as I returned to the kitchen. Once there, I watched discreetly as she walked into the dining room and saw the table.

"Oh, wow. You did this?" she asked, looking

at me.

I'd found her nicest dishes and set the table, taking care of everything so she'd just be able to relax and enjoy dinner. I had carefully moved the puzzle to the very edge and boxed the loose pieces without ruining her system. I smiled and pulled a chair out for her. Again, she looked at me in surprise. Five points.

I served the food, a sliced roast served over an arugula salad. The perfect compromise between Maggie's father's craving for red meat, her mother's desire for salad, and the suffocating heat outdoors. Justin and I chatted through most of the meal, but I kept an eye on Maggie. Every once in a while, I'd catch her throwing me a thoughtful look. It couldn't be that easy, could it?

When we were done eating, Justin immediately stood up and started clearing the table.

"This is ridiculous. This is my house. I can do something," Maggie protested.

"Our house," I said, smiling at her.

"That's what I meant," she mumbled, and then shut up and took another sip of wine.

Mrs. Grant got up to help Justin and Mr. Grant turned to me.

"How was your poker game last night?" he asked.

I lit up, surprised he'd remembered.

"It was great. Thanks for asking. I won the table. First time I'd done that in months," I said.

I couldn't remember the last time someone had remembered some trivial thing about me like that. It felt good.

"Yeah, he was in a great mood last night," Maggie said mischievously.

I reached over and squeezed her arm, rolling my eyes at her for her dad's benefit. Before I could take my hand away, she took in her own and held it for a moment. I could feel the electricity pass between us, and I simultaneously wanted to pull away and stay like that forever. I mentally ran through the reasons why I couldn't touch her and was pissed to discover they still held strong.

I gently pulled away and stood up.

"I'm going to go pack up the leftovers so your folks have lunch for the road tomorrow."

Maggie's dad looked up, pleased. I made my way into the kitchen, but not before hearing him say to his daughter, "I like that one. You chose good."

*

About an hour later, I walked Justin to the

door, following him outside and to his car. I could tell he'd been anxious to get at me all night, so I figured it was best to have it out right away.

"Spit it out," I said.

"What the fuck are you doing here?" he asked.

"I bumped into Maggie the other day, and while we were chatting she got the call from her folks. I offered to help her out."

"So there's nothing going on between you?" he asked, disbelieving.

"There's nothing going on between us," I said.

He looked at me for a moment, then nodded, satisfied.

"But I want there to be."

He reared up and I could see his hand itching to make a fist.

"Relax, man, I don't want to screw her. I like her. I mean, I really like her. I haven't so much as looked at another woman since I met her. Well, not really, anyway," I added, remembering that unfortunate incident in the parking lot of Elena's.

Justin didn't relax his stance, but he didn't make a move towards me, either. So I figured it was safe to carry on.

"I haven't been able to get her out of my

mind. I don't know what it is. But I want to find out."

"She's too good for you."

I laughed.

"You think I don't know that?"

"Then what makes you think you've got a shot? You're a player, Liam. She sees through that bullshit."

I clenched my jaw, willing myself not to say anything I'd regret. This was Maggie's brother. And he had every right to come to that conclusion. I'd provided him with enough ammunition.

"I didn't say I had a shot. But damned if I'm not going to try. Your sister? She makes me want to do better. Be better. She makes me want to be the kind of guy she deserves."

Justin just stood there, staring at me.

"Do you love her?" he asked.

I was silent for a minute.

"If you'd asked me that yesterday, I'd have said no. Now? I don't know, man. I really don't fucking know. I've never been in love."

"I'm not on your team here. But by the same token, I won't get in the middle. You're both adults."

"Fair enough," I said.

He nodded once, got into his car, and drove away. I turned around and went back inside.

CHAPTER TWENTY-SEVEN

Maggie

Liam had been gone a while, considering Justin had been parked right out front. I tried not to give it too much thought as I sat in the living room with my folks. My mom was telling me all about their adventures and every once in a while my dad would interject to comment on a stand-out meal or someone else's RV. I'd never seen them so happy and animated. Maybe the whole RV lifestyle had been the right move for them after all.

Liam walked back into the house a few minutes later, looking suddenly exhausted and maybe a little dejected. I gave him a questioning look but he just smiled and came to kiss the top of my head.

"I think I'm going to turn in," he said. "Long

day, and I'm sure the three of you want to catch up."

I felt a moment of disappointment. After the day we'd had, I had been looking forward to the flirting that was sure to transpire in front of my parents. The more I thought about it, this night was like my bonus round; my one chance to claim the prize.

I watched him leave the room and then turned my attention back to my parents. But the longer I stayed there with them, the more I wanted to head upstairs. I reminded myself it would be a long while, hopefully, before I saw my parents again and with that in mind, I dropped Liam from my thoughts and enjoyed their company.

*

It was close to eleven when my mom finally yawned and told my dad it was time for them to turn in. I carried the empty teacups into the kitchen, hugged them goodnight, and made my way up to the bedroom.

I expected to find him asleep in my bed, having not taken out the mattress, but to my surprise, he was up and pacing. In his underwear. He stopped when he saw me enter.

"I'm sorry," he said, indicating his attire. "I

didn't bring anything with me."

"Right. Don't worry. Nothing I haven't seen before," I smiled and walked toward him.

He backed away and cocked his head.

"Where, uh, do you keep the mattress?" he asked.

Seriously?

"It's out in the hall closet. I forgot about it. It would probably look kind of weird if we went out to get it now. You can share the bed, it's okay," I said, hoping he got my point.

He stopped pacing and looked at me. The air in the room was charged and if I felt it, he must, too. I approached him again, my eyes glued to his chest. *Thank you, Lord, for these gifts I'm about to receive.* I reached out and put my hand on his cheek and he closed his eyes.

I got up on my tiptoes and kissed him gently on the mouth. It felt bold, but it also felt right. It was easy to have no inhibitions when there was nothing at risk. It took him a moment to respond, but he did, and before long we were completely entwined. I moved my hand down towards his waist and he jumped back.

"No, I'm sorry, Em. No."

I started at the use of the nickname. I'd almost forgotten about him using it the last time my folks were here. I'd hated it then. Sounded almost familiar now. But what did he mean, no?

"What do you mean, no?" I asked.

He licked his lips and swallowed, clearly nervous, which instantly put me on edge.

"Are you seeing someone?" I asked, backing away in horror.

"No, no, it's nothing like that. I swear."

"So what is it? We've done this before, you know. Nothing's changed. House rules still apply."

He glanced away and took a moment to collect his thoughts. I watched the muscles in his abdomen move as he breathed in and out. It was a decent distraction. I let him take his time. Finally, he turned to me.

"That's the thing. Things have changed."

"What's changed?"

He let out a long breath.

"I like you. You're a nice person."

I laughed.

"And that prevents you from sleeping with me."

I watched in amusement as the impact of what I'd said hit him. He closed his eye and bit his bottom lip. It was pretty fucking sexy.

"Yes," he said.

I moved away and sat down on the bed.

"Well, if it helps, I kind of like you, too."

He looked at me, hopeful.

"Really?"

"Yeah. You're a decent guy. Great in bed. I mean, what's not to like. Fine, the whole reputation thing, but that doesn't affect us here, tonight. Come over here. Stop overthinking this."

He sat down beside me and took my hand.

"You don't get it. I *like* you."

My heart stopped. All of sudden there was no air in the room.

"Um, can you clarify that last statement, please?"

He sighed and dropped my hand, standing up again and starting to pace.

"What can I say? I can't stop thinking about you. About us. I don't know what it is. I've always just...moved on. With you, I haven't. I want to know more about you. Who you are. What makes you tick."

"Oh."

There was a moment of silence. The enormity of what he'd said wasn't lost on me. This was the same man who'd basically admitted a few short weeks ago that he refused to let anyone in his life.

"You don't feel the same way," he said.

"I just hadn't thought about it. I hadn't thought of you that way, I guess. That sounds horrible, doesn't it?"

He shook his head and sat down again.

"No, it doesn't." He sighed. "Listen, we met under really weird circumstances. And I have zero regrets about what's happened, but if you'd let me, I'd love to try a more, uh, traditional approach here."

"What did you have in mind?" I asked.

"A date?"

Again, I laughed.

"Liam Grayson on a date?"

"That's just the thing. That's who you see me as. I don't want to be that guy with you. Please. Let's start again."

I chewed on my lower lip while I thought about what he'd said. He was *not* my type, but really, did I even know what my type was? All my failed relationships had been with guys I'd deemed my type, and look what happened there. I glanced over at him, taking him in from head to toe, then looked quickly away again. Good lord, he was cute. It made my insides curl.

"Okay," I said. "Close your eyes while I get changed."

*

The lack of the spare mattress meant we still had to share the bed. With this new understanding between us, it made for a very awkward situation. While I didn't particularly have any strong feelings towards him, I was certainly entertaining some thoughts about his body. I shifted under the covers and moved further over to the edge.

"You sleeping?" he asked.

"Nope."

"How's the writing going?"

I smiled in the dark, even though he couldn't see.

"It's finished. The book is done, edited, and on submission at three different publishing houses."

"Maggie! That's fantastic. I'm so happy for you."

He sounded genuinely enthusiastic, and it was nice. I hadn't even gotten that reaction from my parents. My father was more like, "Well, this will be the true test, then, won't it?" It was enough to make me resolve to never discuss the process with them again.

"How's everything going at work?" I asked.

"Busy. Crazy. Unmanageable. I love it."

"I'm sure you do."

"Can I ask you something?"

"Sure," I said.

"Shane? Bookstore guy? Is he anyone—?"

"No. He's not anyone."

"I just want you to know, I haven't seen anyone since—"

"Liam," I said. "Stop. You don't have to explain anything. We just agreed to start again, remember?"

"Right. Sorry."

"Get some sleep," I whispered.

Within minutes, his breathing was following a regular pattern, and I knew he'd drifted off. I, on the other hand, was awake for a very long time.

CHAPTER TWENTY-EIGHT

Liam

I stood at my station, humming along to The Foo Fighters under my breath as I trimmed the steaks for the evening's service.

"I guess things went better last night," Toni said.

"I'm guessing you're right," Tasha agreed.

As usual, Statler and Waldorf were off in the corner discussing me as if I weren't there. I ignored them and kept working. The best part of the song was coming up anyway.

"Did you just do-do-do a guitar solo?" Adam asked incredulously as he walked into the kitchen.

"Screw off, Grohl himself does it in the acoustic version," I said, not even looking up.

He laughed and kept going, eager to join the

group in the corner.

"What did I miss?" he asked.

I dropped my knife, wiped my hands, and turned around.

"Okay. I've had enough. You want details? Fine. Last night was great. I told her how I felt, she agreed to give me a shot, and now I'm just trying to enjoy the fucking day before the fact that I can't pull this off hits me."

Bree walked over and put a hand on my shoulder.

"Hey, give yourself some credit. Not a lot of men would've been able to take that first step. Did you, uh, you know?"

"Fuck her? No. And she offered."

Adam started.

"Seriously, man? I'm impressed. Didn't know you had it in you," he said.

"Yeah, well, I do. We shared a bed and I was a perfect fucking gentleman. You were right. I have to do this the right way." I turned back to my steaks and picked up my knife. "Now someone kindly tell me what the right way is."

*

The next few days flew by. The constant stream of customers coming through the restaurant kept us all busy. Unlike Christmas, when we only opened for dinner, during the summer we served three meals a day. Cottagers were big on brunch, and we knew how to deliver. The addition of summer staff ensured I never had to be in before eleven, so it was a perfect scenario for all involved.

Almost a week after her parents left, I called Maggie and asked her out on a date. I got Sunday night off because I knew neither of us worked on Mondays and I figured if things went well, there'd be no rush for her to get home. If things didn't go well, I was pretty confident she'd have no qualms about letting me know.

"Where are you going to take her?" Bree asked.

"Elena's," I said.

Both Toni and Bree turned to me simultaneously.

"You can't be serious," Toni said.

"Dead serious. She'll see right through me if I try to take her anywhere nice. I can't overdo it with her. She's not starting from scratch. I have to be true to me, but show her that can be a good thing."

"Learn that from one of your novels?" Bree asked, laughing.

"You mean one of *Toni's* novels?" I corrected.

She just rolled her eyes. I turned back to my work.

*

On Sunday night, I drove over to Maggie's to pick her up. I brought her a bunch of wildflowers, which she took graciously and put in a vase.

"Do you want a drink or something?" she asked.

Tempted as I was, I resisted.

"We should probably get to the restaurant. We can do our drinking there."

"Where we going?" she asked.

"Elena's okay?"

She smiled.

"Perfect."

Five points for me.

We left her place and drove out to Highway 4. We talked a bit about work and her folks, but I kept it light. I really wanted to know if she'd heard back from any publishers, but she hadn't offered up the info and I didn't want to cast a dark mood over the evening if the book had been rejected.

She looked gorgeous. She was wearing a green short sundress with a loose skirt and spaghetti straps. Her freckles were outrageous, and I loved every single one of them. I kept glancing over at her as I drove, unable to keep my eyes off her. Shit, I was in trouble.

She was wearing these strappy shoes that went up her ankle. Not a heel really, but a kind of wedge-thing. They made her legs look fantastic and I had made sure to follow her down the stairs when we left her place. It was going to be a chore keeping my hands off her, but I was determined.

I had gone equally casual, wearing a black T-shirt with a pair of jeans. Yet it somehow took me an hour to figure it out. There was a pile of clean clothes on the bedroom floor I wasn't looking forward to folding later.

When we got to the restaurant, I raced around to open her door, but she was already out of the car. I smiled sheepishly.

"Don't try so hard," she said softly.

It was the kindest thing she could've said under the circumstances, and I took it to heart. I still wasn't sure what I was doing there with her. She was so different from anyone I'd ever been with. But I'd never felt this way about any of those women, so maybe that said a lot about my past choices.

We walked into the restaurant and Elena came right over, giving me a hug and offering Maggie a kind smile. I introduced them, and as

Elena showed us to our table, I leaned over to whisper in Maggie's ear.

"That intro will guarantee you a free margarita on every visit."

She smiled wickedly. Ten more points for me. We sat down and Elena handed over the menus.

"Do you think we should do a pitcher?" Maggie asked.

"If you like. I'm good for two, I'm driving," I reminded her. "Depends on how drunk you want to get."

She turned to Elena.

"Pitcher, please."

I laughed.

"Really? Does it take copious amounts of alcohol to enjoy my company?" I asked, only half-joking.

"No. I'm just a little freaked out that I'm even here. I gotta tell you, in a million years I never envisioned this scenario." She leaned across the table and looked at me earnestly. "You could be with any other woman in this room. You know that that. And you'd get laid."

I leaned forward and met her halfway.

"But they're not you."

She blinked.

"You're serious about this. You like me."

"Yes."

She laughed softly and shook her head.

"Part of me only came tonight because I couldn't believe it. I thought I must have misunderstood something last time. You swear you're not playing me?"

I took her hand.

"Maggie, I swear I am not playing you."

She nodded slowly.

"Okay then. I'll have the chorizo tacos."

I laughed. She knew how to break the tension. She also knew how to eat, something I greatly appreciated. I found myself daydreaming about teaching her shit in her kitchen, the two of us prepping meals together on weekend mornings. It might not have been her idea of a good time, but I was already ten steps ahead, picturing what I could do to *her* in that kitchen.

"You still with me?" she asked as our food was set down before us.

Without hesitation, she reached in and picked up her first taco, devouring it in three bites. Most of the women I'd dated would either pick at a salad or insist on a liquid meal. This was fucking refreshing. I dug into my food and we ate in silence punctuated only by the occasional sound of our margarita glasses hitting the table.

The place was busy, but not packed. There

was a steady stream of 90s hits coming through the jukebox, and some counselors from a local summer camp on their night off were dancing on the makeshift dance floor.

"I love this place," Maggie said.

"Me, too. The food is A1, and the atmosphere is off the charts. She's really built something here," I agreed.

"You know, I order something different every time I come. I never do that. I'm the kind of person who picks a favourite for each restaurant and sticks to it."

I smiled.

"That explains why you've ordered the mushroom risotto each time you've been to my place."

"Exactly. I mean, I'm sure everything is delicious, but once I've found something I like, why not go with a sure thing?"

"Jesus, Maggie. Because there's so much more out there to try. Maybe you'll like something else equally as much. Or even better. That's it. You never get to order in my restaurant again. Chef's choice. I'm telling Toni."

She laughed, delighted, and I took another swig of my drink. The evening was going well. If only I could keep my eyes off her mouth.

CHAPTER TWENTY-NINE

Maggie

I was having a good time. There was no denying it. The physical attraction was still strong, but for the first time, I forced myself to put that aside and focus on Liam, the man. And I found him to be curious, attentive, and engaging. I was pleasantly surprised.

I was a drink ahead of him, and I was feeling okay. When The Wallflowers came on, I put down my glass and looked him straight in the eye.

"Dance with me," I said.

He smiled and got to his feet, putting out his hand for me. He led me onto the dance floor and pulled me into his arms. Together, we swayed to the music, him holding me close. I lay my head on his shoulder, enjoying the feel of his hands on my back, his scent enveloping me.

"This is nice," he said quietly.

"Mmmm."

"I never dance. I wonder why," he mused.

"Maybe it didn't seem manly enough to you?" I teased, looking up into his face.

"Fuck that, this is awesome." He pulled me in closer and I laughed against his chest.

He tried a little spin, and it would've been successful if I'd been steadier on my feet, but after three margaritas, that wasn't the case. We collided with the couple next to us and I burst out laughing, Liam bringing me in once again to keep me out of harm's way. Or for everyone else's protection.

We stayed on the dance floor for quite a while. He was graceful but clearly unpracticed. It was charming, and I appreciated that he was trying. The slow songs were the best, when his arms would come around me and everyone else just melted away.

"Hey, you okay?" he whispered in my ear.

"Yeah, I'm good."

"A little wobbly, I think. Should we go get some air?"

I giggled and shrugged, following him outside into the parking lot. It was a gorgeous night, a slight breeze bringing the temperature down a little. Nights were always cooler up north, but sometimes in late July and early August, even those were unbearable.

"This was an excellent idea," I said, spreading out my arms to the sky. "Look at that sky."

Liam stood behind me, hands on my shoulders as we star-gazed.

"Do you know the constellations?" I asked.

"No, I wish I did. You?"

"No. We can learn them together."

He let out a soft laugh.

"I'd like that."

I turned to look at him over my shoulder.

"The date's going well, don't you think?" I asked.

"I do. I'm glad you think so, too," he said, brushing a stray lock of hair out of my face.

"You know, usually when a date goes well, the guy will try for a kiss."

I closed my eyes and waited, but nothing happened. I opened one eye, only to find him staring at me, amused.

"You're not going to kiss me," I said.

"You're drunk. And I'm trying to be a gentleman."

"What if I don't want you to be a gentleman?"

I heard a groan coming from somewhere

deep in his chest.

"Please don't say that."

I turned around and laced my hands behind his neck.

"Kiss me," I said.

He gently took my hands and brought them back down to my sides, not letting go of me. He looked me right in the eye.

"Let's be clear about something," he said. "I want to kiss you. Very much. But you are drunk, and I'm working too hard here to fuck this up. And if we can get through this part, then believe me when I tell you I will kiss you. And I won't be a gentleman about it. I have not forgotten what you look like when you come."

I felt a rush of heat between my legs and I squeezed my thighs together. Every nerve ending in my body was alive and dancing, aching for his touch. A touch I knew wasn't coming.

"Can we go home?" I asked.

"Absolutely."

We walked silently to his car, and he unlocked the door to let me in. Then he got in, started the car, and stared straight ahead for almost a full minute. Then he turned off the engine.

"Are you mad at me?" he asked.

I shook my head.

"No. But what are our options here? Go back inside and suffer from this sexual tension, or say goodnight and look forward to the next time we meet?"

He turned the key and we pulled out onto the highway.

*

"Not even a kiss?" Tammy asked.

"Not even a kiss."

"Liam Grayson? Liam Grayson objected to kissing you because you were drunk?"

I nodded my head and continued folding towels. I was standing in the hallway on the third floor beside my hospitality cart and Tammy was pacing the hallway, getting all the details of my Sunday night date. She'd tried calling me on Monday, but my hangover was unbearable and I hid under the covers all day.

"That's unbelievable. Who are you, woman? What kind of power do you possess?"

I laughed and started pushing the cart towards the next room. Tammy followed close behind, not yet satisfied.

"When are you seeing him again?" she asked.

"Wednesday. He's coming over to make me

dinner."

Tammy waggled her eyebrows at me.

"Returning to the scene of the crime?" she asked.

"Please. We're going to have a nice dinner, maybe watch a movie. Completely innocent."

"Yeah, right." Tammy checked her phone and slipped it into her pocket. "I've got to get downstairs. My shift starts in five. We'll pick this up later."

*

Wednesday rolled around fast, and I spent the entire day in a daze. My supervisor pulled me aside twice, and I apologized profusely before getting back to work. This was ridiculous. I was a grown woman who had a date with an attractive man she'd been fake dating and almost slept with and who was now interested in pursuing a real relationship with her. There was absolutely nothing to be nervous about.

And yet.

I managed to get through the day, get home, and shower before Liam rang the bell. I'd just slipped into a black tulip skirt and fitted white T-shirt. I hadn't even had time to pull my hair back. I went downstairs and opened the door to find him standing there, two paper shopping bags under his arms. I grinned and moved aside to let him in.

"You look fabulous," he said as he passed me.

Huh. He was getting more and more chivalrous as time went on. I'd been under the impression it was supposed to go the opposite way. I followed him into the kitchen, watching as he unpacked the groceries he'd clearly swiped from the restaurant. He looked larger than life in my kitchen, tall, broad-chested, tattooed. His jaw moved slightly as he worked, and he occasionally chewed on his lower lip. I'd never noticed either of those things before.

"What are we having?" I asked.

In response, he pulled two lobsters out of one of the bags. I jumped back.

"Those are alive," I said.

"Yes, they are. Don't worry, I'm about to kill them."

"Jesus Christ."

Liam burst out laughing, dropping the lobsters in the sink as he came over to me.

"You've never made lobster?"

I shook my head, wide-eyed and maybe a little terrified. What if they got out of the sink? How fast did lobsters move? Did they bite?

"No. I like eating it though. I'm thinking maybe I'll go change or something—"

"Don't change."

"Well, I don't want to be here while you, you know…" I made a slicing motion across my throat and cocked my head towards the sink. Liam just laughed.

"They can't hear you."

I let out an exasperated sigh.

"Just let me know when you're done, okay? We'll eat in the dining room. I'll go set the table."

I turned around and left him to his own devices. He certainly knew where everything was. I turned my back on him and hummed loudly as he worked. I could hear him filling the pot with water and briefly wondered where the lobsters might be. I thought it was a good time to fluff the pillows on the couch.

By the time I heard the screams, I was refolding the blankets I stored in the ottoman. I sat down hard and counted to ten. He'd just murdered two lobsters in my kitchen and they were screaming.

"They're not screaming," he called out, reading my mind. "It's just the air escaping their shells. They were dead before they hit the water."

I wasn't sure that thought was any more comforting.

I made my way back to the kitchen and

retrieved a bottle of white wine and two glasses. I poured, then handed one to him.

"To second dates," he said.

I raised my glass to meet his and took a sip, looking up as I drank.

"What's on your mind?" he asked.

"Nothing. No, that's not true. I was just thinking how much I was looking forward to this evening, and how that's surprising and not surprising all at once."

"Elaborate," he said.

I took a deep breath, exhaled, and took another sip of wine before answering.

"Well, when we met, I was a little intimidated by you. Then, I thought you were just a superficial guy, you know? Nothing there. But the more time we spent together, the more I learned the truth. You're a good guy, Liam. You're smart, funny, well-educated. You're killer at your job. I can't figure out why you'd sell yourself short all these years in the relationship department."

He just shrugged.

"I don't know what to tell you. That was just the game. The life of a chef. Work hard, party harder. It never occurred to me that they could be two separate things: my career and my private life. Until I met you."

He turned back to the counter, picked up his

knife, and continued chopping vegetables.

"Do you want me to help?" I asked.

"Nah. Just keep me company."

I turned on some music and then just stood there, sipping my wine and watching the muscles under his shirt flex as he worked.

CHAPTER THIRTY

Liam

I felt her eyes on me as I worked, but I was confident enough in my skills that I didn't let it shake me. I was able to go on autopilot when necessary. And it was necessary. All I wanted to do was drop the knife and take her in my arms. I should've taken her dancing again. There was no way I'd get away with a cheesy move like dancing with her in the kitchen.

"Any news on the novel?" I asked.

I'd debated bringing it up, but I hadn't brought it up last time and I worried if I didn't ask this time I'd look like I'd forgotten, or worse, didn't care. I knew it was a risk if the news was bad, but I had a backup plan to cheer her up if required.

"Nothing yet," she said. "Thanks for asking,

though. Sweet of you to remember."

I was racking up the points tonight.

I got everything together, plated our meals, then followed her out to the dining room, where she'd set a beautiful table. There was a beautiful bouquet of tulips in a vase. *Shit.* I forgot to bring her flowers.

I put down our plates, then pulled out her chair. Once seated, I pulled out a linen lobster bib I'd brought and tied it on for her. She laughed delightedly.

"You think of everything, don't you?" she asked.

"Apparently not everything," I murmured.

"What?"

"Nothing."

I walked around to my seat and sat down, tying on my own bib in the process. She looked at her plate, then up at me in awe.

"I can't believe you can do this with your hands."

"Oh, there are a lot of things I can do with my hands."

It just slipped out, but she blushed and grinned mischievously. It was worth it.

We made casual conversation over dinner. I commented on her new jigsaw puzzle. She filled me in on the various guests staying at the hotel. It was a lot of the same celebrities who had been eating at the restaurant. In such a small town, it was hard to avoid that kind of overlap. I asked about her parents, and Justin, and whether she was writing anything new.

She lit up when she talked about her writing. She had a new novel in the works. The marinating stage, she called it. I listened as she talked about the characters and her idea for the story. She came alive in those moments—there was a fire in her eyes that wasn't there when she talked about anything else. I kept asking her more and more questions to keep her talking. It was a fucking joy to watch.

She did interrupt from time to time to ask me questions, too. I answered them, but briefly. I didn't want to be curt, but I also didn't want to monopolize the conversation. Every one of those damn books had reinforced this point.

We cleaned up together after the meal.

"I can't believe how amazing that was. Thank you," she said.

"It was my pleasure, really. I love to cook. Even when I'm off. Job hazard, I guess."

"Don't look at it like that," she said. "You're lucky to do something you love and get paid for it."

"True. You're a hundred percent right."

We made our way into the living room and she grabbed the remote before taking a seat on the couch. I hesitated only a minute, then sat in the armchair. I just didn't trust myself.

"What do you want to watch?" she asked.

"Honestly? Can we watch that movie you started the first time I was here? I could never remember the name and we didn't finish it and I always wondered what happened to the kid —"

She burst out laughing, turned on the TV, and found the movie. I loved that she didn't tease me about it. I glanced over at her as she was tucking her legs up under her. She caught my eye and grinned. I couldn't take my eyes off her.

"Liam," she said. "Get over here. Come kiss me."

I flew off the chair and onto the couch in less time than it took her to blink. Taking her face in my hands, I leaned down and lightly brushed her lips with my own. She moaned softly and I did it again, this time using my tongue to gently part her lips. She wrapped her arms around my neck and crawled into my lap. I felt like I was home.

I don't know how long we sat there, making out. At one point, she pulled away, looked at me with pleading eyes, and said, "More."

I just shook my head.

"Let's just take this slow. This is so fucking

good, Em."

It was almost light out by the time I left. My balls were aching and I had no idea how I was going to make it through the day, but fuck, it had been worth it.

*

I was out with Adam at a nearby farm, picking up eggs and dairy products. It was a beautiful day and I was in a great mood. Forty-eight hours had passed since my last date with Maggie, and I was still on a high from that make-out session. I must have been humming under my breath.

"Sounds like it's really going well," Adam commented, as we loaded crates of eggs into the back of his truck.

"I think it is," I said. "We had a great time the other night. I think she saw me for the first time."

Adam nodded.

"I remember what that was like with Tess. Man, it was hard to win her over. Of course, I came with the added baggage of a kid and a broken heart."

Adam had been widowed some years before, and he and Tess had gotten together last winter, despite her protests that she wasn't the family sort. I thought about it as we got into the car, how completely that woman's life must have changed when they hooked up. She was basically my female equivalent in Mountain Valley, except she'd been living there longer.

I saw her often, of course. She was always at the restaurant. She seemed happy. Happier, in fact. I used to bump into her at parties and shit. She was never my type, but we ran in some of the same circles. I thought maybe I should chat with her.

"You got quiet," Adam remarked.

"Yeah. Sorry. Just wandered for a moment there. How'd you know she was the one?"

He took a minute before answering.

"I don't know if you ever know. I think it's about trusting yourself, letting yourself feel."

"Helpful."

"Listen, Chef, here's the thing. You like the girl, see where it goes. It doesn't have to be forever. You're dating. You like her. Just take it from there. Don't overthink this."

Now that was solid advice.

By the time we got back to town, it was near noon. Toni had taken care of lunch and I was due in the kitchen. Adam and I parted ways at the door and I spent the next several hours head down in the weeds. Friday nights at Cagney's were off the hook and it was always a rush to work the dinner crowd. I didn't come up for air until close to eleven, and when I checked my phone, I saw a bunch of missed calls from Maggie.

I walked outside into the parking lot and called her back. She picked up after the second ring.

"Liam?"

"Maggie. What's up? Something wrong?"

"I got two rejections today."

She sounded like she'd been crying.

"Oh, shit, Em. I'm sorry. That must sting."

Sniffles. Yup. She was crying. I had never dealt with a crying woman before, and I wasn't quite sure how to handle it.

"Listen, Maggie, I'm just finishing up my shift. Do you want me to come by?"

"Please. That would be great."

I shoved my phone back in my pocket and went back into the kitchen to change out of my work clothes.

"Where you going?" Bree asked, poking her head in. "You're not joining us at the bar for a drink?"

"Not tonight," I said.

She smiled knowingly and backed out of the kitchen. I grabbed my stuff and left. On the walk over there, I thought about how Maggie had reached out to me in a moment of distress.

I felt a vise-like grip on my heart and stopped for a minute to catch my breath. This was what I'd wanted, right? A relationship with this woman. This is what a relationship was. Being there for each other. I swallowed and broke out in a cold sweat. *Don't be ridiculous, man.* I shook it off and kept walking.

CHAPTER THIRTY-ONE

Maggie

I hesitated for a long time before calling Liam. We'd just started dating, and I had no idea where we stood with each other. But I was crushed, and I wanted him close. Somehow, this seemed like something Tammy couldn't help me with. No one could *help* me with it, but I felt if anyone could understand what this meant to me, would be able to comfort me, it would be Liam. If he wanted a chance, this was his chance.

When I didn't hear back, I freaked out a little and left him a message. I tried him a few more times before realizing it was a Friday and the restaurant was probably crazy. I felt like an idiot. He'd think I was a stalker or something.

Now here I was, pacing the living room,

waiting for him to arrive. When the first rejection came in, I was disappointed. It hurt, but I felt I could deal with it because there were still two more chances. When the second one came in, I just burst into tears. Sue at work covered for me and I took the rest of the day off.

The bell rang and I stopped pacing, taking a deep breath to centre myself before greeting him. Behind my disappointment, I could feel the excitement at seeing him, and it brought the first smile of the day to my lips. I glanced down at my shorts and T-shirt, then walked over to open the door.

"Maggie."

He pulled me into a hug and brushed back my hair with his large hand. It felt divine. I could have melted into him.

"You okay?" he asked.

I shrugged.

"I will be. It's just, you know?"

"I know. Come, let's go inside. I brought you some desserts."

I smiled and led him into the living room, where we both got cozy on the couch before he pulled three take-out containers from a paper bag, all containing chocolate delights. I grabbed a plastic fork and dug in.

"That's better," I mumbled between bites.

He laughed and stretched his legs out on the ottoman, closing his eyes.

"I'm sorry," I said. "You're probably exhausted. And I dragged you over here."

He shook his head but didn't open his eyes.

"Nowhere I'd rather be," he said.

I reached over and touched his hair. He opened one eye and smiled at me before closing it again.

"Just give me a minute," he murmured.

I leaned over and put the container down on the ottoman, then crawled into his lap. He let out a small pleasurable groan as I ran my fingertips down the side of his jaw before bending down to kiss him.

"Em—"

"Shhh..."

I wrapped my arms around his neck, deepening the kiss until he responded. Before long, his fingers were threading through my hair, his hands running down my back. He kissed the soft spot under my ear, then the side of my neck before reaching the hollow place at my collarbone. I clutched his T-shirt as his head dipped into the V of my neckline.

"I like those noises," he murmured.

I hadn't been aware I was making any.

I grabbed the hem of his shirt, pulling it up over his head and tossing it to the ground. I buried my face in his chest, inhaling his scent before exploring the landscape with my lips and tongue. His hands worked quickly, tearing off my shirt and unclasping my bra. I pulled it off, letting my breasts fall against his bare chest as he kissed me again. Every inch of me was on fire. I wanted him more than I'd ever wanted anything.

I repositioned myself in his lap, grinding into him as I felt him grow hard beneath me.

"Em, fuck—"

"I want you. Please."

"Shit."

He lifted me off his lap with ease, depositing me on the couch beside him. He dropped to the floor before me, tugging at my shorts as I raised my hips off the couch, letting him slide them down my legs along with my panties. He traced one finger between my legs and I arched my back, eager for more.

"You're so wet," he groaned. "Em, you're so —"

I pushed his head down, feeling a boldness I'd never known before. He spread my legs apart with his hands, peppering the insides of my thighs with light kisses. I was squirming, trying to align his tongue with my target, but he was having none of it, teasing me until I thought I would scream. Until I did scream.

"That's what I was waiting for," he said before burying his head between my thighs, using his tongue to take me places I'd never been. I held his head with one hand and clutched the couch pillow with the other, riding his face as licked and sucked, pushing me close to the edge.

"Liam," I breathed. "I'm so close."

He slid his hands under my ass, squeezing hard as his tongue worked its magic. I opened my eyes and looked down at him, watching him devour me. It was so incredibly sexy, both of us moving, his hands and mouth all over me. He reached up and cupped my breast and I closed one of my hands over his as I raised my hips off the couch, chasing my release.

"Yes, Liam, that's it. Oh my god. Oh, shit. Liam—"

The orgasm broke over me like a tidal wave, and I held onto him so hard I probably left bruises. But he wouldn't stop, kept kissing me, licking me, stroking me with his tongue. I wrapped my legs around his neck, pulling him in closer, pressing myself against his face.

He reached up and slid one finger inside me, and I exploded a second time, crying out his name as I came. This time he let me rest, kissing the insides of my thighs as I came down. Then he reached for his jeans and pulled out a condom. He glanced up at me, questioning, and I nodded.

I took his wrists and pulled him back up towards me, leaning in for a kiss. I took the condom from his hands, tearing the foil and pulling it out. He dipped his head to trace a circle around my nipple with his tongue. Whenever his mouth made contact with my skin, it was like fireworks in my brain. He short-circuited me, and I couldn't think straight anymore.

I reached down and took him in my hand, stroking him gently but firmly until he started to moan. Then I slipped the condom on and lay down on my back on the couch. He grinned and took my hand, pulling me up to my feet. He grabbed me by the hips and lifted me, prompting me to wrap my legs around his waist. He kissed me as he walked me to the dining room table, onto which he gently deposited me.

"Not a missionary guy," he whispered in my ear.

My insides melted.

He pulled me towards the end of the table and slid himself into me in one fluid, practiced move. Then he stilled, staring at me, wonder in his eyes. Without a word, I understood exactly what he was thinking. Never had I felt anything so exquisite, so incredible, so—

"Shit, Em."

"I know, I feel it, too."

"Hold on."

I put one hand on his shoulder and grabbed the edge of the table with the other as he began to move inside me, slowly at first, then increasingly faster. I braced myself, using my leverage to raise my hips and meet each thrust, angling myself for maximum friction. The table shook, puzzles pieces falling to the ground.

There we were, both of us, naked, having sex, in my dining room with the lights on. It was unlike anything I'd ever done before, anything I'd ever felt before. I wanted that moment to last forever, him gazing into my eyes, his face awash in pure pleasure.

I felt the orgasm building, slowly, steadily, lazily. It was just out of reach, teasing me just as he was, pulling out and waiting for me to whimper before sliding back in. My body was electric, sending off sparks in every direction. I closed my eyes and threw my head back, abandoning myself to whatever was to come.

He dipped his head, taking a nipple in his mouth and biting lightly as he continued to thrust. His pace was controlled, but I could tell he was close. I could feel it in the way he moved, the way his hands seized my hips.

"Come for me, Em," he whispered.

I opened my eyes and looked down at the place where our bodies joined, then looked back at him through hooded eyes. I reached down, finding that spot that I knew would drive me over the edge. He increased his speed as I increased mine and together we sailed over the edge, him swearing, me calling out his name.

CHAPTER THIRTY-TWO

Liam

The moment I closed her front door behind me, I knew I'd made a mistake. Whether the mistake was having told her how I felt, sleeping with her, or sneaking out in the middle of the night, I wasn't sure. But a mistake had been made.

I'd been crazy to think I could pull this off. That I could be boyfriend material. She'd needed me and I freaked out. I'd almost had a panic attack on the way to her house. And then how did I comfort her? With sex. Classic Grayson. Maggie deserved better than that. Better than me.

I'd been planning to go home, but I found myself heading towards Franni's bakery. I had toyed with the idea of talking to Tess about all this, how she coped with the abrupt lifestyle change. I checked the time. It was close to six o'clock. I knew someone would be there...with any luck it would be Tess.

I could smell the baked goods before I even turned the corner onto Main Street. No one else was around yet, save for the occasional jogger and dog walker. The door to the bakery was open and if it had been a cartoon, there'd have been visible steam wafting into the street.

I walked in and saw Jax behind the glass wall, working away in the kitchen. I poked my head in.

"Hey, Liam. How you doing?" he asked, pausing to look up from his tray of danish.

"Unsure. Is Tess around?"

He laughed and slid the tray into the waiting oven.

"No. She doesn't show up until close to noon. You telling me she and Adam don't keep the same schedule? We figured that was why she'd changed her shift."

I thought about it and realized he was right. Adam had been coming in around noon these days, save for the occasional times there were extenuating circumstances...like a farm trip. They hadn't been together long, but they seemed to have already carved out a little schedule for themselves.

"Right. Okay. Hey, listen. Does she seem, uh, happy to you?"

He looked up, shocked.

"Tess? Yeah, why? What have you heard?"

"No, no, it's nothing like that." I was quick to reassure him. The last thing I wanted to do was start rumours. "This is actually about me."

Jax put down the towels he was using to hold the hot trays and walked over to me. He jumped on the stool, grabbed two croissants, and handed me one.

"What's up?"

I took a step back. I hadn't exactly been planning on having a heart-to-heart with another dude. But he was just sitting there, waiting for me to say something. I opened my mouth, then shut it again. Should I tell him? It kind of made sense, Jax was also a player, just for the other team. But he'd never really settled down with anyone, at least for as long as I'd known him. And in such a small town, I'm sure I would've heard if he'd had his heart broken at some point in the past.

I pulled up another stool and tore off a piece of the croissant.

"I think I fucked up."

"Tell me."

So I did. And when I was done, he was staring at me, a look of combined pity and amusement on his face.

"So you just walked out? While she was sleeping?" he asked.

"Yeah," I said. "It's fucked up. I know. I screwed around with her, then I decided I liked her, figured I'd never get her, got her, and then took off."

Jax contemplated this for a moment.

"Maybe it was just the chase?" he suggested.

"I don't think so. Every time I think about her, I want to throw up."

"Is that supposed to be a good sign?"

I jumped off the stool and started pacing.

"I don't fucking know. No woman has ever gotten into my head like this before. When I woke up and saw her lying there, next to me, my fucking heart stopped. I just panicked, and I fled. And the more I think about it, the more I think I did her a favour. Look at me, I'm a fucking mess."

"Hey, relax. You're just a little freaked out is all. Let me get you a cup of coffee."

Jax took off into the front of the bakery to the coffee machine. I paced the floor, trying to figure out how I came to be standing in Franni's kitchen at six o'clock in the morning talking about my love life with a man I'd never exchanged more than a dozen words with.

I heard the jingle of a bell and looked

towards the front door to see another guy, Chance I think, come in. He shot a questioning look at Jax as he made his way to the kitchen.

"Hey. Chef Liam, right? From Cagney's? Man, I love your food."

I smiled and took his outstretched hand.

"Yeah. Chance, right?"

He nodded, seemingly please I knew his name.

"Let me know next time you're in the house. I'll come say hi," I said.

He smiled and went to get washed up and into his apron. Jax returned and handed me a coffee, holding one for himself.

"I made it black," he said.

"Wise."

I took a sip. It was good coffee. I took a longer sip and let it slide down my throat, ignoring the burn. I deserved it.

"Listen, I'm no expert at this, but all I'll say is, figure out what you really want. You've lived one way for a long time. A challenge came along. Like I said, maybe you just liked the chase? Who knows. Figure it out before you screw with her head anymore, though. Maggie's a nice girl."

"Yeah, I know that. I know I'm not good enough for her."

"Shit, man. No. It's not like that. If you like

her, and she likes you, that's all that's important. But it seems like you won her over, and now you're not sure what to do with your prize. That's the shit you've got to figure out."

Huh.

I took the last sip of my coffee before throwing the cup in the trash.

"Thanks, man. That was really helpful. Come by for dinner sometime. My treat."

Jax smiled and Chance's head shot up.

"Yeah, yeah. You, too."

I walked through the bakery, out the door, and headed home for a few hours of sleep.

CHAPTER THIRTY-THREE

Maggie

"He was just gone?"

"Yeah."

"No note?"

"None."

I was hiking one of the more challenging trails with Tammy as I told her about my night with Liam. I'd texted her the moment I woke up and we both called in sick. Might've looked suspicious, but I didn't care. This was an emergency.

"What the actual fuck is that?" she asked. "Who does that? Well, I guess Liam Grayson does that."

I didn't even know what to say. I had no idea what had happened, what, if anything, I could've done to provoke his leaving. I'd thought we'd had a great night, despite the fact I'd been crushed about the rejections. The sex had been mind-blowing. At least, for me. Maybe it hadn't been for him? No. Impossible. We were both there.

"Maybe he got scared?" I mused.

"Fuck that shit," she said. "No. No one treats you like that. Fuck him."

"You think?"

"I do."

We hiked on in silence for a while. Pushing myself physically was the only way I was managing not to cry over this entire thing. If Tammy was right, and he was just an asshole, where did that leave me? How stupid had I been to trust him? After everyone, including my own brother, had told me not to trust him. I had been willing to just screw around, dammit, and he'd insisted on getting to know each other, saying he liked me. What the hell?

"Do you think he was just being cruel?" I asked, terrified to hear the answer.

"I don't know. I don't think so. That's just beyond, don't you think? You were there for the taking. He knew that."

"My thoughts exactly. Should I call him?"

"NO!"

Tammy's shout echoed through the forest and we both stopped and laughed. It was a nice break in the tension, something I hadn't realized I'd needed.

"Hey," she said. "I've got an idea. Why don't we go away? There's a great band playing in Rocky Heights tomorrow night that I'd love to go see. We're both off Monday. We'll stay the night and make a little vacation out of it."

"And how do you propose we get away with that?" I asked.

"Don't worry. My manager owes me a favour, and she's friends with your supervisor. Let me ask if they can re-arrange the schedule tomorrow. I'll tell them it's an emergency."

"That sounds like a great idea."

*

Tammy worked her magic and Sunday afternoon we were in her car, driving through the mountains towards Rocky Heights. She'd scored tickets to the show, some metal band performing outdoors. I'd balked, telling her I was not a metal fan, but she told to me hold off on any judgment until I saw this act perform. Whatever.

I turned up the radio in the car and tried not to reflect on the fact that Liam had made zero attempts to contact me. It had been 36 hours since I'd last seen him, flushed from sex, collapsed in my bed. We had been at it for hours. I didn't even know I was capable of so many orgasms. We moved through my house until we ended up in my bed, both of us spent, exhausted. And then I woke up alone.

"Fuck men," I said.

"Yeah, fuck men," Tammy agreed. "We can do that tonight if you like."

I threw her a look.

"I think I'm done with that for a while," I said.

"Oh, come on, don't let one bad apple spoil the cake."

"I don't think that's how that expression goes."

"I like cake."

I laughed as we pulled up to the hotel. Tammy found parking and we grabbed our overnight bags before heading in. The place was packed. I was shocked Tammy had managed to book us a room, but she'd explained that there was a network of hospitality workers in our area. I guess I just hadn't been around long enough to find out about it.

"This is weird. It's my first time staying in a hotel since I've been working in one," I said, dropping my bag on the bed. "I almost feel bad about sleeping in the sheets."

Tammy laughed.

"I always try to be extra nice at check-in. Job hazard, I guess. Come on, let's get changed and find some food before the show."

*

Tammy was right. Hammer of Thor was amazing. It was a perfect night—clear sky and a slight breeze. The crowd was enormous and thrumming from the band's energy. It was unlike any concert I'd ever been to before. The ability to scream and move with complete abandon did wonders for my psyche. It was like the entire event was set up as a cover for me to release my frustration over Liam.

We stayed pretty far back from the stage to avoid the crazy mosh pit, but when the show ended Tammy flashed me a smile and grabbed my hand. She led me to the backstage area where she pulled out a pass that she'd obtained from God knows where and the security guard ushered us behind the rope.

I glanced down at my outfit - a short skirt with a crop top and a pair of sandals. I was very casual in comparison to Tammy, who was decked out in a pink off-the-shoulder dress. It would've been nice to have some warning, but

I took it in stride and made a note in my mental friendship book: *Always ask Tammy what to wear.*

There was a lot of action behind the stage, but Tammy navigated it like a pro.

"I'm a summer groupie," she confided as we weaved through the crowd.

"Every day it's something new with you," I laughed.

I saw the band up ahead and elbowed Tammy. A grin spread across her face and she grabbed my hand and led me over.

"Billy!" she shouted.

One of the security guys turned and saw her, breaking out into a big smile as he walked towards us.

"Tammy. Was wondering when you'd show up. Good to see you."

The two exchanged hugs and he led us towards the band.

"Hey, guys, this is Tammy and her friend—"

"Maggie," I interjected.

"Maggie. Fine ladies. They just wanted to say hi." Billy bowed his head and moved back to his post.

Tammy walked straight up to the guitarist and put out her hand.

"Hey, Damien. I'm a huge fan."

Damien was tall, olive-skinned with long

brown hair that hung to halfway down his back. He was fierce-looking, tattoo sleeves on both arms and a large silver ring on his finger. He took Tammy's tiny hand in his own huge one and shook it warmly.

"Pleasure to meet you, Tammy," he said.

Tammy almost swooned and I put my hand on her back for support. She shot me a glance and smiled.

"Maggie and I were just wondering what you guys were up to. You heading to any of the bars?"

Damien shook his head.

"Straight to the casino. Got a spot waiting at the poker table."

I snapped to attention and looked at him again. Heavy metal, poker player...

"Uh, do you by any chance know a Chef Liam Grayson?" I asked.

Maggie glared at me.

"Liam! Yeah, I know that dude," he said, laughing. "He made us a kick-ass meal on tour a few years back. Great guy. You know him? Tell him I say hi."

I shook my head in disbelief. No matter what I did, I couldn't escape. My desire to party was rapidly diminishing, but Tammy took note and pulled me aside.

"Hey, we are going to the casino and we're

going to have a good time tonight. Fuck him, okay? Let's go drink and dance and hang with some rock stars."

I pulled myself together and forced a smile.

"Let's have at it, then."

CHAPTER THIRTY-FOUR

Liam

"You did what now?" Toni asked, glaring at me with a very large knife in her hand.

I back away a few steps and put my hands out.

"Listen, I just completely freaked out. She called me upset, I went over there. I'm not used to playing the boyfriend. Things got a little out of hand, and, well, I bolted."

"This was when?"

"Saturday morning," I said quietly.

"SHIT, Chef. It's Tuesday. What the fuck is wrong with you? No wonder you've been in a shit mood all weekend."

I shrugged.

"I told you I wasn't good enough for her."

"You weren't fucking kidding."

Toni put down the knife and started pacing, too angry to even look at me. Bree poked her head in to ask a question, saw the scene playing out, and stepped cautiously through the door.

"What's going on?" she asked.

Toni stopped and looked at her.

"Oh, nothing. I just asked Chef about his day off and he casually mentioned fucking Maggie on Friday then taking off in the night," she said.

Bree whipped around to glare at me. Now I had two fierce women pissed at me. This was not going to be a good day.

"Listen, in my defense, I did try to get in touch," I said.

"Please, for the love of all that's holy, tell me you didn't text her," Bree said.

"Of course not!" I said, indignant. "I went over there. She wasn't home. I even went by the hotel, but they told me she'd taken a few days off."

"You try calling her?" Toni asked.

I shook my head.

"No. After that, I just lost my nerve. I fucked up. Better to just walk away from the whole thing. I don't want to drag her into my fucked up life."

"Your life is not fucked up, Chef. You just don't know how to do relationships. And neither does she. This is something you can do together if you give it half a chance," Toni said.

She'd calmed down enough to pick up her knife and resume chopping. I stood by the stove, watching my sauces simmer and reduce. I wasn't so sure she was right.

*

When my shift was done, I got into my car and started driving. I wasn't sure where I was going until I found myself heading towards Highway 4. A margarita seemed like a good idea.

I pulled into the parking lot at Elena's and made my way inside. The place was packed for a Tuesday night, and once again I thanked God for the tourist season. There was a crowd of people around my age at the bar so I made my way over. I instantly recognized a few faces, seasonal renters who were regulars at the restaurant, and the rounds starting coming.

By eleven o'clock, I'd forgotten my troubles and was having a great time. Fuck it all. This was who I was meant to be. Where I was meant to be. Out drinking after a hard day's work, not consoling some woman over a book deal gone wrong. I was not that guy.

Even if maybe I wanted to be.

"Hey, can I get you another drink?"

I looked over and saw Greg, the bartender, awaiting my answer. I nodded and he grabbed my glass, instantly replacing it with a fresh scotch. The night was young, and I could always cab it back if necessary. There was a cute blond on my right, and I turned my attention to her.

"Hey. Liam," I said.

She smiled and put down her drink to shake hands.

"Rebecca. You don't recognize me?"

I paused and studied her for a moment, trying to remember if I'd slept with her, but no bells were ringing.

"I'm sorry. I don't. Is that horrible?" I asked.

She laughed, a melodic little sound that made me smile, and put her hand on mine.

"No, it's not. I was in your restaurant a couple of nights ago."

"Ah."

The relief must have been plain on my face because she burst out laughing.

"Did you think we'd slept together?" she asked.

I grinned sheepishly and shrugged.

"Listen, you're really cute, and things have been known to happen," I said.

She swiveled around on her stool and

crossed her legs, looking directly at me.

"You're a flirt," she said.

"That accusation has been leveled previously, yes."

"Buy me a drink."

"It would be my pleasure." I turned to the bartender. "Greg! Can you get Becca here another of whatever she's drinking?"

Greg nodded and got to work mixing the drink. I turned back to see her grinning wickedly.

"Becca?"

I shrugged again.

"Suits you."

"So tell me, Chef, what brings you out all alone on a Tuesday night?" she asked.

"I was hoping to meet you."

"Oh, that's bad. Wanna try again?"

I thought about it for a moment as I took a swig of my drink.

"I'm getting over a broken heart."

She cocked her head and studied me.

"Well, that I believe."

"Do you? I'm not so sure."

"You've never had your heart broken before?" she asked.

"Didn't even know I had one," I answered honestly.

"This sounds serious. Tell me."

She signalled Greg for another round so I downed the rest of my drink.

"Ever read romance novels?" I asked.

She burst out in shocked laughter.

"Actually, I do, why do you ask?"

"I somehow found myself in the classic scenario of fake- relationship-turned-real."

Once articulated, it felt like a huge weight had been lifted off my shoulders. Crazy as it sounded, that was exactly what had happened. And once I realized it hadn't been my fault, that I'd been thrust into the situation and things had just taken a turn, I understood why I'd been freaking out. I was a man in control of my destiny, but after meeting Maggie, I had lost that control.

"You're kidding, right? How does that even happen?" Rebecca asked.

I snapped back to attention and looked at her as if seeing her for the first time. This had clearly gone from a pick-up situation to a therapy session, but I was oddly okay with that. Possibly even relieved.

"Well, it was kind of like this..." I proceeded to tell her the entire story, from start to finish, as we went through several more rounds of drinks. By the time I was done, we were both drunk off our asses. She laughed at something I said and slipped off her stool. I reached out to grab her arm, and she held onto me as she righted herself.

"Interesting."

I turned around to put a face to the familiar voice and there stood Tammy, shooting daggers at me with her eyes.

"Tammy!" I said. "Hey. How are you?"

"Clearly not as good as you are, Chef."

She turned on her heel and walked out of Elena's. *Shit.*

CHAPTER THIRTY-FIVE
Maggie

I know what you're thinking. You're wrong. Please call me.

I sat on the bed in 315, staring at my phone, trying to calm my nerves. It had been four days since Liam had taken off in the middle of the night. Four days of me wondering what I did wrong, or worse, what was wrong with me, that he split immediately after sleeping with me.

I went away with Tammy. We partied with the rock stars. I threw myself into work. But nothing I did could stop the questions running through my brain 24/7. Like hamsters on the goddamn wheel, they just wouldn't stop.

And then that morning, Tammy told me she'd seen him drunk off his ass with some woman at Elena's. And now this text. How could he possibly know what I was thinking? I didn't even know what I was thinking. Four days and he made zero effort to contact me, and now this.

There was a gentle knock on the door and I looked up to see Tammy standing there, a sympathetic look on her face.

"How you doing?" she asked.

I held out my phone for her and she walked over, took it from my hand, and looked down.

"This is the first you've heard from him?" she asked.

I nodded.

"I don't know what to tell you, Mags. I know what I saw. They were together the entire night at that bar."

"I just don't understand why, after taking off like that, he'd even feel the need to explain anything. Maybe I should hear him out."

"I don't know. I agree you've got a point, but he didn't even call you. Not once. You checked that damn phone every five minutes. Maybe he's got a guilty conscience? Maybe he just wants to fuck with you some more? I don't know. I'd let it sit. Honestly."

I stood up and tucked the phone into my pocket. I went out into the hall to get fresh towels and finished making up the room.

Tammy just sat and watched me, that same concerned look on her face.

"You can go back to work, Tammy. I'll be fine. I promise I won't do anything stupid."

She nodded and stood up.

"Okay, but come get me at the end of your shift. We'll walk home together."

I smiled and she walked out of the room. I had a dozen more rooms to get through before three o'clock rolled around, so I put in my headphones and got busy. By the time I was done and got downstairs, Tammy had already signed out for the day, was changed, and was waiting for me.

Leslie, who worked the evening shift at reception, smiled when she saw me.

"Maggie. Glad I caught you. I kept meaning to come find you. That hunky chef from Cagney's? He was in here a couple of times over the weekend looking for you."

My heart dropped. I looked at Tammy and we just stared at each other, shocked. I swallowed and put my hand on the reception desk to steady myself.

"He did what now?" I asked, just to be sure.

"He came by. A few times. He seemed really desperate to see you. I didn't want to tell him you'd left town, but I also didn't want him to keep coming by. He just looked so dejected. I hope you're not mad."

I shook my head slowly.

"No. Not mad," I assured her.

Tammy came over and took my hand, smiling over her shoulder at Leslie as she guided me out the door, onto the street. I took a deep breath of fresh, albeit humid, air.

"You okay?" Tammy asked.

"Unsure," I said.

"Understandable. I'm sorry if I gave you any shitty advice. This kind of changes everything, doesn't it?" she asked.

"Yeah, I guess it kind of does."

"I guess you're formulating some sort of plan?"

I nodded. She leaned over and kissed the top of my head.

"I'll see you tomorrow. Good luck. Call me if you need me."

*

My first stop was the restaurant.

"He's not in," Jen said. "He called in sick this morning. Sorry, Maggie."

I wrangled his address out of her and left, heading straight for the deli. I picked up a bacon-and-cream-cheese bagel and a pint of chocoholic ice cream. I didn't know what his hangover cure was, but that combo had always worked for me.

I made my way through the centre of town until I found his building. I stood there for a moment, wondering what to say when I buzzed up, but a woman came along and opened the door. She turned to me, questioning, and I smiled, grabbing the door from her before it shut.

I climbed the stairs to Liam's apartment raised my fist to knock. I took a deep breath, licked my lips, and gave myself a quick pep talk. What was really the worst that could happen? I knocked.

I heard a bang inside, followed by swearing, as he made his way to the door. I held my ground.

"Who's there?" he called.

I opened my mouth but nothing came out. I was suddenly incapable of speech.

He threw open the door, an angry expression on his face which vanished the moment he laid eyes on me. If I hadn't seen the transformation myself, I never would've believed it, but in that single moment, I had no doubt how he felt about me. Whatever his actions had been. I couldn't help but smile.

I held out the bag with the bagel and ice cream.

"I brought you my hangover cure," I said.

Relief flooded his face. He dropped to his knees and wrapped his arms around my legs. I took him in in all his hungover glory—loose sweats, no T-shirt, day-old growth on his jaw. If this was him at his worst, I was all in. I was already imagining the feel of that stubble against my inner thighs.

"Maggie. Maggie. I'm so sorry."

"You just split."

"I know."

"You really fucked up."

"God, I know."

"What happened?"

"I think I got scared. Fuck, Maggie. I really like you, but I've always been in control, you know? And all of a sudden, I wasn't. But in those four days apart, man, I gotta tell you. I think when it comes to you, I don't mind losing control. So long as it means not losing you."

He got to his feet and I dropped the bag, throwing my arms around his neck. Our lips met, and I swear it was like coming home again. It just felt right. Not to mention damn good.

He licked my lower lip and slipped his tongue into my mouth. I deepened the kiss, pressing myself up against him, feeling the muscles in his shoulders under my fingertips.

God, it was amazing just to hold him in my arms, feel his body against mine. I could've stayed like that forever. He pulled away.

"You're still wearing your little maid uniform," he said, an evil twinkle in his eye.

I looked down, realizing I'd never bothered to change after my shift. Once I heard he'd been by looking for me, my goal was single-minded. I laughed and looked up at him.

"Fantasy of yours?" I asked.

He shrugged.

"It is now," he said. "Come, come inside."

I followed him into the living and stopped dead. The coffee table, armchair, and even the floor held piles of paperback novels. I reached down and picked one up. *Small Town Love*. I picked up another. *His Fake Bride*. I turned to him, stunned.

"You've been reading romance novels?"

He nodded. I surveyed the room.

"How many of these have you read?" I asked.

"All of them."

I blinked.

"Why?"

He grinned, looking suddenly very shy.

"I wanted to be, well, I wanted to be the man you deserved."

I was speechless.

"Don't you get it, Maggie? You completely turned my world upside down. This started as a favour, one I didn't particularly want to do if I'm being honest. But then you walked into my life. And you made me laugh, and you're so fucking sexy, and you just made me feel things I hadn't felt before. It confused me. It wasn't who I thought I was."

He walked over, slowly.

"But I like who I am with you. And I hated who I was when I walked out on you. When we're together, Maggie, it's unlike anything I've ever experienced. And I don't just mean in bed. Although I do mean that, too."

I laughed. He leaned down and kissed me softly before continuing.

"I want to be everything for you. I thought these books could teach me something."

"You don't need them, Liam. I like you. These men—" I waved vaguely towards the stacks of novels. "They're not real. You know that. Real people are going to make mistakes. I make mistakes, too. I promise."

"I guess I couldn't quite bring myself to believe that," he laughed.

"Believe it."

I took his face in my hands and kissed him. He reached behind me and pulled the string on my apron, letting it fall to the floor. I twined my arms around his neck, getting on my tiptoes as he unzipped me. He gently pushed down on my shoulders, forcing my arms to my sides as he slid the uniform down until it, too, dropped to the ground. I stood there before him, in nothing but my bra and panties, my breath catching as he ran one fingertip down the front of my body, making a circle around my navel as my insides clenched.

"You're gorgeous, Em," he whispered.

I closed my eyes.

I felt him draw closer, until there was only an inch or two between us, that space quickly becoming charged. I let out a slow breath as he took my chin in his hand. His mouth closed on mine and I put my hands on his hips, sliding my fingers into the elastic waist of his sweatpants. He groaned against me and I pushed down, letting his pants fall around his feet. He was wearing nothing underneath. I may have whimpered.

I closed my hands around his ass, pressing my hips into his as he kissed me, feeling him grow hard against me.

"You missed me," I observed.

"You have no idea," he growled.

I wrapped my legs around his waist as he lifted me and walked us through the living room and into his bedroom. He lay me down on the bed, kneeling over me to peel down my panties, tossing them across the room. He inhaled deeply, staring at me with pure lust in his eyes.

"I hope you don't have any plans for the rest of the day," he said. "This might take a while."

I took his head and pushed it down between my thighs. With no further ado, he got to work. As his tongue worked its magic, I couldn't believe there'd ever been a time where I thought I wouldn't enjoy this. That I could do perfectly fine without it.

As Liam's tongue teased my clit, I knew I'd never been more wrong in my life. I raised my hips off the bed, already racing towards the edge. He wrapped his lips around me, sucking gently and I grabbed onto his shoulders, holding on as I thrust into his face. He squeezed my ass with one hand, bringing the other between my legs and sliding two fingers inside me.

"Oh, fuck, Liam," I cried out.

I felt him smile against me and I opened my eyes to look down. He raised his own eyes, meeting my stare and the desire in them was overwhelming. This man, this beautiful man, wanted me. I grabbed his head and threw my own back against the pillow as he increased the pressure. I was a speeding train, racing forwards, nothing able to stop me. I cried out as I came, clutching his hair as I rode out the waves of the orgasm.

When I came down, he raised his head got on his hands and knees, crawling up until he was positioned above me. I put my hands around his waist, pulling him down closer, needing contact between our bodies. He leaned over and pulled open the night table drawer, pulling out a condom which he dropped on the bed beside us.

"You're not going to leave this time?" I asked, only half-joking.

"It's my apartment," he grinned.

CHAPTER THIRTY-SIX

Epilogue

"You up?" Liam asked.

"Nope."

"Come on, wake up," he insisted, gently poking me in the side.

We'd been together six months, living together for four. In all that time, not one morning had passed that I hadn't woken up to the smell of fresh-brewed coffee coming from my kitchen. This morning, there was no such aroma.

"You know what I need," I said.

"Shit, Em, didn't we just do that a couple of hours ago?"

"Ha, ha. You know what I mean."

I cracked an eye open and looked at him. He was standing by the side of the bed, one hand behind his back.

"I think this is more important than coffee," he said.

I sat up, suddenly wide awake. This was very un-Liam-like behaviour.

"What's up?" I asked.

He pulled a large envelope from behind his back.

"You got mail," he said, handing it over.

I took the envelope, looking at the front. It was addressed to me, and the return address was the last publishing company I'd submitted to. I was up to seven rejections at this point and had just about given up. I took a deep breath, opened the envelope, and pulled out its contents. I studied them for a moment before looking up at Liam. There was an anxious look in his eye.

"It's a publishing contract," I said, in shock.

"YESSSS!" he screamed, doing a victory lap around the bed before taking a giant leap and landing in his spot next to mine on the mattress.

He grabbed me, pulling me into an enormous bear hug. I laughed, unsure of what felt better—receiving this incredible news, or the fact that I had someone to share it with who was just as excited as I was. I pulled him down with me into the pillows, burying my face in the space between his shoulder and his neck. My most favourite spot.

"Get up, I'll take you to brunch and we'll celebrate," he said.

I lifted my head and peered out the window into the January winter wonderland that lay outside.

"I don't know," I said. "Looks cold. Why don't we do our celebrating right here?"

He grinned wickedly and smacked my ass.

"What exactly did you have in mind?" he asked.

"Well, I'm working on this scene in my new book. Not so sure about the feasibility of it..." I reached down into the waist of his sweats and found him hard and ready for me.

"I think I get the picture," he said, his voice husky.

I tilted my head up for a kiss and he obliged. I stroked him, and he worked his pants off before reaching up to cup one of my breasts. I was still naked from our early-morning romp, after which I'd fallen into a deep sleep. Monday mornings with Liam were the best.

"That feels—" I started, but he cut me off with another kiss.

His hands were everywhere and my body was on fire. No matter how often we had sex, it was never enough. My thirst for him was unquenchable, and from the way he devoured my body, I knew he felt the same. He bent his head and took one nipple in his mouth, sucking gently as I moaned. His hand worked my other breast and my head was spinning. He slid his other hand down below my waist. I was so wet his finger just slid in, easily finding its way to the magical spot that sent me off into orbit.

"I want you in my mouth," I managed to get out.

He got to his knees by my head, his hand still working between my legs. I reached up and took him in my hand, stroking him a few times before reaching out with my tongue to taste him.

"Oh, god, Em."

I wrapped my mouth around him, sliding my tongue up and down and I pulled him deeper into my throat. I felt his knees buckle before he reached over with his spare hand to brace himself against the wall. His thumb found my clit and he pinched lightly before starting to rub me rhythmically, driving me towards a sure orgasm. He'd gotten to the point where he could make me come in under two minutes. But once he'd done it, he'd refused to do it again. No, Liam much preferred teasing me, drawing out my pleasure.

My hips came up off the bed and I cupped his balls, squeezing lightly as I traced a line up his shaft with my tongue. He increased his speed with his thumb as he started to fuck my mouth. I looked up at him and our eyes met, his hooded and shining with desire. I exploded into my orgasm, surrounded by bright colour and intense waves of pleasure as he pulled his cock out of my mouth, repositioning himself on top of me.

"For a guy who doesn't do missionary," I said, "you seem to do a lot of missionary."

"I fucking love watching your face when you come on my cock," he growled, leaning down to bite my neck as he slid into me.

He thrust once, twice, and then stilled. I used the opportunity to roll him over onto his back, never breaking our connection, as I straddled his waist. I grabbed his hands and put them on my breasts. He needed no further instruction as I started to ride him.

"Was this was you had in mind?" he asked.

"Almost," I panted.

I lifted my hips, letting him slide out as I swung one leg over and repositioned myself so I was facing his feet.

"Ah, the good old reverse cowgirl," he laughed.

"This has a name?" I asked.

"Still so much to teach you. You know, for a romance writer, fuck—" He stopped talking the moment I slid back onto him. I couldn't blame him. The angle was exquisite.

I started to move, slowly at first, then picking up speed. The length of his cock slid along my clit as I rode up and down, and I reached down, applying more pressure with my hand, increasing the sensation until I was a puddle of moans and soft cries.

I felt his hands on my back, and then they slid around cupping my breast, squeezing as I rode him. I could feel his control, his refusal to move his hips and let me set the pace. The power I felt was undeniable. It was definitely an aphrodisiac. I had never been so turned on in my life.

"Liam?" I said.

"Yeah?"

"I think I'm going to come."

He pinched my nipples, sending me flying over the edge. I grabbed hold of his thighs as I rode it out, crying out over and over until I felt him pull me firmly against him as he came deep inside me. We'd ditched the condoms months ago, and the feeling when he came inside was often enough to make me come again. He reached around, finding my clit and rubbing frantically, knowing he could get me there.

"Oh, fuck, Liam," I screamed as I came a second time. I collapsed forward, my breasts against his thighs, as I tried to regain my breath. His hands moved slowly over my lower back, my ass, finding the place where we were still joined and running his thumb along it. I sighed happily, once again awed that we'd ended up together.

*

"Hey, Em, phone for you."

I walked into the kitchen, going over the contract in my hands, to find Liam holding out my cell phone. I must have left it there the night before. I hadn't even heard it ring. I'd fallen back asleep, once more, after our celebratory session and had woken to the smell of pancakes and bacon.

I padded over and took the phone from him, putting it to my ear.

"Hello?"

"Sweetheart! It's your mother. How are you?"

I shot Liam a dirty look and he just smirked, turning back to the stove.

"I'm fine, Mom. How are you?"

"I'm well. Your father, too. We decided to

spend this cold day planning our spring and summer travel plans and guess what? You're first up on the itinerary. I'm giving you plenty of advance notice so you can take the time off."

I took a deep breath in before replying, but then decided not to argue. Why bother? I had a publishing contract in my hands, literally. Who knew if I'd even be working at the hotel in four months? Maybe I'd be able to write full time.

"Why don't you give me your dates and we'll see what we can do," I said.

"Well that sounds lovely. I will do that, dear. Any chance Liam can get some time off?"

I glanced over at him, remembering how he'd handed me the phone without warning.

"Pretty sure that can be arranged," I said.

"Fabulous. I mean, it was a nice visit last time, but with the two of you running in different directions all the time, we didn't get enough time together. I mean, really, Maggie, you never even told us how you got together in the first place."

I burst out laughing and sat down at the kitchen table. Liam put a plate in front of me before sitting down to his own.

"Actually, Mom, that's a really funny story. Have you got a minute?"